"Until I Can Prove My Innocence I Have Nothing To Offer You."

"You can offer yourself. That's all I want."

He shook his head. "You're dreaming, Leda. This isn't some romantic play where the hero and the heroine solve everything neatly by the curtain. This is real life, and in real life I'm a dead end, a loser, a convicted felon with no future and no prospects. Go home, Leda, and forget me."

"I can't forget you, and I won't," she replied, blinking back tears. "I want to feel the way you made me feel this morning. I want you to kiss me again and make me forget everything but us. I'm willing to fight for what I want. And I want you."

Dear Reader,

Welcome to Silhouette! Our goal is to give you hours of unbeatable reading pleasure, and we hope you'll enjoy each month's six new Silhouette Desires. These sensual, provocative love stories are both believable and compelling—sometimes they're poignant, sometimes humorous, but always enjoyable.

Indulge yourself. Experience all the passion and excitement of falling in love along with our heroine as she meets the irresistible man of her dreams and together they overcome all obstacles in the path to a happy ending.

If this is your first Desire, I hope it'll be the first of many. If you're already a Silhouette Desire reader, thanks for your support! Look for some of your favorite authors in the coming months: Stephanie James, Diana Palmer, Dixie Browning, Ann Major and Doreen Owens Malek, to name just a few.

Happy reading!

Isabel Swift
Senior Editor

SDRL-7/85

DOREEN OWENS MALEK
Winter Meeting

Silhouette Desire

Published by Silhouette Books New York

America's Publisher of Contemporary Romance

SILHOUETTE BOOKS
300 E. 42nd St., New York, N.Y. 10017

Copyright © 1985 by Doreen Owens Malek

Distributed by Pocket Books

ISBN 0-373-05240-5

First Silhouette Books printing October 1985

10 9 8 7 6 5 4 3 2 1

America's Publisher of Contemporary Romance

Printed in the U.S.A.

Books by Doreen Owens Malek

Silhouette Romance

The Crystal Unicorn #363

Silhouette Special Edition

A Ruling Passion #154

Silhouette Desire

Native Season #86
Reckless Moon #222
Winter Meeting #240

Silhouette Intimate Moments

The Eden Tree #88
Devil's Deception #105

DOREEN OWENS MALEK

is an attorney and former teacher who decided on her current career when she sold her debut novel to the first editor who read it. She has been writing ever since. Born and raised in New Jersey, she has lived throughout the northeast and now makes her home in Pennsylvania.

One

Snow blew across the windshield and gathered on the frozen grass as Leda Bradshaw turned the car into the narrow, dirt-packed lane. It threaded through the brown lawns, thickly frosted now with white, as the grave markers on either side of the passage rose out of the storm like sentinels.

"It's the last one on the right," Aunt Monica reminded her.

"I remember," Leda answered quietly, slowing the car to a stop near the marble memorial. She had never been back to see it since her father's funeral. And now this year she was back in Yardley on the anniversary of his death, and Aunt Monica had talked her into the visit, hoping to exorcise the ghost that had haunted Leda since the sudden loss of her parent. And somehow, with Aunt Monica along, the prospect did not seem as terrible as it had in the past.

They got out of the car and turned toward the forest of markers, the sounds they made muffled by the wind and the driving, drifting snow. The storm had enhanced the effect of early winter dusk, and it was almost dark as Leda made her way to her father's grave. Aunt Monica followed on her heels, her boots silenced by the powdery carpet beneath her feet. A twilit hush had settled over the cemetery, and the sighing of the wind in the trees and the hiss of falling snow combined to enclose the two women in a still, breathless world. On such a day it was easy to believe that the sleep of the dead who rested there was peaceful.

Leda stopped short as she caught sight of her family's name. A magnificent spray of holly decorated the grassy mount in from of the marker.

She turned to the other woman. "He always loved holly, Aunt Monica. Thanks."

"I cut it from the bush out by my patio," Aunt Monica said. "I put it there last week, on Thanksgiving." She studied Leda's absorbed expression. "I'll leave you alone for a few minutes."

Leda nodded, her eyes on the carved lettering and the numbers below, which delineated the short years of her father's life. Such a brief span of time, and now it was over. All that remained was a handful of ciphers on a stone slab, and a single mourner on a raw December day. Her vision blurred with tears as Aunt Monica walked off into the trees. Leda moved closer, wiping her eyes with a gloved finger. It was several seconds before she realized there was a man standing on the other side of the grave.

Leda halted in surprise. He was half turned away, standing at a distance from the memorial, as if he didn't want to approach it too closely. It was an odd time of day for a visit, but more important, she had thought she knew all her father's friends. She didn't recognize this man, who stood half in shadow, his collar turned up against the chill.

He obviously wasn't aware of her presence. Leda's approach had been silent, cushioned by the snow, and something indefinable kept her from calling out to him. He moved slightly, stepping into the light from an overhead lamppost as he jammed his bare hands into his pockets, and she got a better look at him.

He was tall and slim, but not too slim, with broad shoulders and a lean, graceful build. He seemed to be in his middle thirties, and was dressed too lightly for the weather, wearing only jeans and a shirt and an ancient leather flight jacket. This was of an indeterminate dark color, worn to gray at the seams, softened with age and use, unzipped to the waist. A beige wool scarf was draped ineffectively around his neck, doing nothing to keep him warm, but he seemed impervious to the cold. He stared fixedly at something on the ground before him as snowflakes settled on his clothes and hair.

Leda remained motionless, fascinated. Who *was* this man? His expression was grief-stricken, as if her father had meant something to him and he missed him. He had to be here for her father; they were at the end of the row and there was no other grave close by. Leda could see only the visitor's profile, but it was handsome, if a trifle severe, with a strong nose and a straight, uncompromising mouth. His hair was dark, deep brown or black, and the melting snow caught in its thick layers made it glisten with silvery moisture.

He'll catch a cold, Leda thought. His hair is wet and he's wearing only those thin-soled running shoes on his feet. As she watched he bent and retrieved the object he'd been studying. It was a bunch of late-season flowers, asters and marigolds and mums, blazing amber and russet and gold against the white blanket of snow. He carefully arranged the waxed paper covering around the blooms, his face intent and serious.

Leda walked toward him, waiting for him to notice her. He didn't. She was almost on top of him when she reached out and touched his arm.

The man started visibly, as if he'd been wrenched away from painful thoughts. He whirled to face Leda, who withdrew her hand as if burned. He looked down, and she looked up; he was very tall. His eyes were gray, the cold gray of a bullet casing or the windswept gray of a bleak November sky. His lashes were long and curling, like a child's, with sparkling snowflakes caught on the tips. His face, full on, was as spare as his profile, with high cheekbones and a firm, chiseled mouth. His aspect was one of strength and determination rather than conventional good looks, but the effect on Leda was unmistakable. She froze as her gaze locked with his.

The man's lips parted. His eyes, their ebony pupils surrounded by rings of platinum, searched her face, and Leda saw comprehension dawn in them. He knows me, she thought with sudden insight. Why don't I know him?

Aunt Monica's voice pierced the silence. "Leda, what are you..." The words trailed off into nothingness as she saw Leda's companion. The man glanced at the older woman, and his face went blank. In one swift movement he dropped the flowers on the grave and stepped past Leda, moving toward the road. He turned once, to meet Leda's eyes again, and a shiver went through her at the intensity of his gaze. Then he strode swiftly away. The snow enshrouded his departing figure as Leda and her aunt looked after him.

Leda stared into the distance for some seconds after she could no longer see him. Then she turned to her aunt, who was looking in the same direction, her eyes narrowed, her mouth drawn into a prim line.

"Who was that?" Leda asked. "Aunt Monica, do you know that man?"

Her aunt faced her in surprise. "Don't you?"

Leda shook her head, hugging herself as a sudden gust cut through her clothes. "But whoever he is, I feel sorry for him. He looked so sad."

Aunt Monica made a disgusted sound. "Don't waste your pity on him, my dear. He doesn't deserve it."

"Why not?"

Aunt Monica's plump face puckered with distaste. "Leda, that was Kyle Reardon, the man responsible for your father's death."

Leda steered her car off the town road and into the paved driveway of her aunt's house. Her tires cut through the two inches of fresh snow on the asphalt, disturbing the perfection of the vanilla frosting surface. She stole a glance at Monica, who stared straight ahead, her hands clamped firmly on the large purse in her lap.

Leda sighed. "I don't think he meant any harm, Aunt Monica," she said gently.

Monica snorted. "How would you know? You were away at school when the whole thing happened. In my opinion, that man is capable of anything. I can't believe he had the nerve to come to your father's grave. You'd think even a jailbird would show more respect. Fresh out of prison and already up to no good." Her fingers tightened on the leather strap she held, and she tossed her head contemptuously.

Leda bit her lip as she slowed the car to a stop next to her aunt's back door. Monica had been fuming about Reardon's presence in the cemetery all the way home. Leda was almost glad to be dropping her off at last. She could use a break from the woman's tirade.

"I don't know what he's doing back here anyway," Monica muttered. "Doesn't he know he's not welcome in this town?" She yanked savagely on the side handle and snow billowed in through the open door.

"He served his sentence," Leda said shortly. "You can't prevent him from taking up his life again."

Monica sniffed. "I would if I could," she responded. She peered at Leda in the dim yellow light shining from her kitchen window. "Are you sure you won't come in for a cup of coffee, or some hot chocolate? It's so cold. Or maybe you should spend the night. I don't like the looks of this storm."

"I'll be fine, Monica. It's early yet, and it's only two miles back to my place."

"Call me when you get home," Monica persisted.

Leda smiled indulgently. "All right." This behavior was typical of Monica. Leda's mother had been Monica's sister, and ever since her death when Leda was a child, Monica had filled in for her sibling with a vengeance. After Leda's father died also, Monica became worse. She found it hard to accept the fact that Leda was a grown woman in pursuit of a career, and still reminded Leda to take her vitamins and wear her galoshes in wet weather. Leda loved her, but occasionally found her fussbudget ways a trial.

"And go home the back way, avoid the bridge. It'll freeze before the road," Monica said, delivering her parting shot as she got out of the car.

Leda waved in agreement, waiting for Monica to enter the house before backing out of the driveway. Monica was a widow who lived alone, since Leda had resisted all the older woman's attempts to convince her niece to stay with her. But although Leda insisted on her independence she worried about Monica, who was in her sixties and no longer as agile as she once had been. Leda didn't pull away until she saw the porch light go out.

Leda deliberately concentrated on negotiating the slippery streets, avoiding all thoughts of Kyle Reardon until she was safely home. She parked her car in the street and scuffled her way through the snow to the door of the duplex she shared with a local art teacher. Leda would have to get up early to dig out her car in order to make her audition first thing in the morning. She unlocked her door, noting that Claire's lights were out, indicating that she probably wasn't home yet.

When Leda's father's business had folded after his death, she'd salvaged enough after paying his debts to buy the duplex. She occupied half of the building and rented the other half to Claire. The rent had kept her going between acting jobs more than once, and she was happy she'd heeded her lawyer's advice to invest in real estate.

Leda removed her boots on the porch and unlocked the door in her stocking feet. She stepped into the living room and switched on the lights, dropping her coat wearily on an armchair. She headed for the kitchen to call Monica and make a cup of tea.

Once she'd hung up the phone and put the kettle on the stove, Leda couldn't stop thinking about Kyle Reardon. She'd been a teenager at the time of his trial, living at a girls' school out of state, but she vividly remembered the tide of feeling that had risen against her father's former employee. Monica and the rest of her family had kept Leda sheltered from the controversy, making sure she stayed at the private school far from home. But since that time the name *Reardon* had become synonymous in Leda's mind with *destroyer*, with *enemy*. The enemy had been faceless until today.

Leda didn't recognize the man because she'd never seen him. Years ago she had managed a peek at some newspaper photos, but those were grainy and poor, with an uncooperative subject. It was no surprise that the man she'd encountered in the graveyard had appeared to be a stranger.

But Monica knew him. She had remarked to Leda as they were leaving the cemetery that prison hadn't changed Reardon much. He still had the look, the manner, the presence, that had deceived Leda's father and everyone else.

Leda couldn't argue with that. She had stood face-to-face with him for only a few moments, but she remembered every glance, every movement, every gesture, of his with a crystalline clarity she would not have thought possible. Never in her life had a chance meeting with another person left such an indelible impression. She was shaken by the experience, unable to dismiss it from her mind. As she moved about the kitchen making a snack, she reviewed what she knew about the man who had ruined her father's business, and his life.

Eight years earlier Reardon had been a test pilot with her father's aeronautical engineering company. He had been working on developing a new jet fuel that wouldn't catch fire in the event of a plane crash. Headstrong and ambitious, but brilliant in his field, Reardon had a reputation for flashes of insight coupled with an incautious nature. He became convinced that his fuel was ready to be tested in flight, but Leda's father disagreed with him. According to testimony given at the trial, Reardon waited until Leda's father was out of town and then ran the test anyway, without the top man's permission. The test failed and the robot plane exploded, killing several of the onlookers. The shock of the accident that resulted in the deaths was so severe it caused Leda's father to suffer a fatal heart attack almost immediately. Reardon, as the responsible party, was indicted for criminal negligence and involuntary manslaughter in the deaths at the testing site.

Leda was only seventeen at the time, but she remembered that Reardon was blamed for all of it, and convicted at his trial. His appeals took a couple of years, but he finally began serving his sentence after he lost the last one. Monica had told Leda that Reardon had just been released from prison the previous week.

Leda filled a mug with hot water, watching the tea bag stain the liquid until it gradually became the color she wanted. Reardon didn't look like a monster, she thought as she tossed the used bag in the trash. He looked like a man to be reckoned with, all right, imposing and memorable, but not quite like the ruthless

opportunist Monica described. But then, how much
could she really tell from an encounter that had lasted
only a few minutes? Intuition and hunches didn't stack
up too well against the mountain of evidence that had
sent Reardon to jail.

Leda glanced at the clock above the stove and re-
solved to make it an early night. She had to catch the
6:53 train from the Yardley, Pennsylvania, station into
New York for her audition. It was a test for a shampoo commercial, and almost certain to be a disappointment. Leda had the requisite shimmering blond
hair, but so did a hundred other actresses, and one
could never be certain what the advertiser had in
mind. In the past few months she'd been deemed too
tall or too short, too heavy or too thin, too pretty or
not pretty enough, and on one disconcerting occasion, "not clean enough." Alarmed at this report,
Leda had been relieved to hear that this meant she was
considered "sexy" rather than "wholesome." The
product to be pushed was white bread, and apparently sexy didn't cut it.

Leda made a face at the muffin she was slicing.
Commercials were hardly the theatrical triumphs of
her college dreams, but they paid the bills. She would
much rather be doing Shakespeare in the park than
extolling the virtues of lemon fresh detergent, but she
had to start somewhere and she had to keep from
starving before she got where she desired to go. The
life of an aspiring actress was a ton of legwork and a
truckload of rejection. Even if she got the commercial, it would do nothing to make her employable the
next time around. Then the advertiser might be looking for a plain Jane to demonstrate a sinus headache,
or a perky brunette to smack her lips over chicken

soup. So Leda kept her hand in doing stage work. It didn't fill her pockets, but did give her the experience she would need in order to interest producers on and off Broadway. After her audition in the morning, she had to make it back to Pennsylvania in time to do the matinee of *Picnic* at the Bucks County Playhouse in New Hope. She had signed for a six-week run ending in January, and she was just settling in and beginning to enjoy herself.

Leda considered herself lucky to be appearing in the production at all. Her agent had initially sent her out to read for the role of Millie, the tomboy kid sister in the play. It was actually a better part than the lead and it was the part Leda wanted. But the casting director took one look at Leda's leggy figure and golden tresses and cast her as Madge, the hometown beauty queen who falls for a charismatic drifter. When Leda protested, showing up for rehearsal the next day in braids and fake glasses, a baseball cap jammed backward on her head, the director had laughed and told her to give up. She was going to play Madge, and Leda wound up doing just that. No one in the audience would accept her as the bookish, intellectual Millie, even though Leda herself was closer in spirit to Millie than she ever was to Madge. But acting was playing "let's pretend," and so Leda pretended, six times a week and twice on Saturday, recreating an August weekend in smalltown Kansas for the denizens of a Delaware Valley winter.

Leda rinsed her empty cup and set it on the drainboard. Her thoughts drifted away from her career and back to Kyle Reardon, like the needle of a compass returning to its pole. Reardon hadn't spoken a word to her, but the communication between them had been

instant and complete. Leda resembled her father very
much; Reardon had recognized her from that resemblance, and from her presence at the grave. What
might he have said to her if Monica hadn't interrupted? Forgive me, I'm sorry, I never meant to do
any harm? Leda knew from the accounts she'd read
that Reardon had maintained his innocence throughout the trial, claiming that he had received permission to conduct the test, and that his fuel had been
sabotaged. Apparently, no one had believed him.

All of those involved—the jurors who had convicted him, the judges who had denied his appeals, the
police and the press and the public—had thought him
guilty. Maybe her emotional response to Reardon's
undeniable attractiveness was influencing her opinion. Compelling men could be criminals too.

She didn't know what to think. The man had
brought flowers to her father's grave, in the dead of
winter, a few days after his release from prison. Why?
The act itself was touching, almost pathetic. It was the
awkward gesture of someone uncomfortable with the
niceties of custom but determined to do something
positive, something right. But when he reached his
destination, he had thrown the flowers away. Did he
feel himself unworthy of the offering, as Monica believed? He certainly hadn't looked happy; his gray eyes
had been haunted, the eyes of a man who lived with
pain and had come to accept it.

Leda shook her head briskly, chasing the topic of
Kyle Reardon from her mind. She had to concentrate
on the audition in the morning, and her performances for the rest of the week.

She left the kitchen and headed for her bedroom,
intent on studying her lines for the first act. The di-

rector had a problem with Leda's interpretation of the
second scene, and she was going to prove to him that
she was right.

Leda didn't get the commercial. She was told her
hair didn't bounce properly, and was sent home. On
the way back to Yardley, she stopped off in the rest
room at the train station. She stared glumly at her reflection in the fly-spotted mirror. Her bounceless hair
lay in still profusion on her shoulders, the reason for
her most recent failure. Leda shook it back in disgust
and studied the rest of her features. They were even,
well proportioned, giving her the sort of looks most
other women envied, but which were almost a disad-
vantage in obtaining the serious roles Leda craved. She
wanted to play Rosalind and Lady Macbeth and Stella
DuBois, and she was usually stuck with the flashy,
fluffy parts for which the shapely blonde was type-
cast. She'd even lost out on Juliet in her high school
play because the English teacher casting it envisioned
the youngest Capulet as a striking Italian brunette.
Leda shrugged. There was always tomorrow, and she
had learned to be philosophical about the vagaries of
potential employers. Maybe she would be lucky next
time.

She had a quick lunch back at her apartment and
changed her clothes, then headed north to New Hope.
Her little green sports car followed the familiar river
road almost by rote, and she observed with real pleasure the snow-whitened scenery as she drove along.
Leda disliked warm climates where winter never came;
despite the ice and traffic hazards, it was her favorite
season.

The parking lot at the playhouse was empty except for Elaine's gray Volkswagen. Elaine was a local seamstress, a friend of Monica's who was coming in early to refit Leda's costumes. She worked part-time as a fill-in wardrobe mistress for the playhouse, which couldn't afford a real one. As a consequence, the actors had to accommodate her schedule. The two fifties-style dresses that Leda wore on stage were too big, cut for the actress originally slated for the part. She had backed out when she got that sought-after holy of holies in the acting profession, a steady job. It was a contract role on a New York-based television soap opera, and she had left New Hope the same day, leaving Leda with outfits for a shorter, slightly heavier girl. Leda pulled in next to Elaine's car and got out, hurrying toward the back entrance of the theater.

The building had a picturesque location on a small waterfall of the Delaware River, and the sound of the gushing torrent filled Leda's ears as she climbed the wooden steps to the rear porch and let herself inside. She made her way down the narrow corridor to the wardrobe room. Elaine was waiting for her inside, tapping her foot, her measuring tape in hand.

"Come on in and let's get going," she greeted Leda. She was never one for elaborate preliminaries. "Get out of those jeans."

Leda obeyed, stripping quickly and standing in front of Elaine in her underwear.

"Look at that waistline," Elaine sighed. "I haven't seen my ribcage in twenty years."

Leda smiled to herself. Elaine's fondness for ice cream would keep her ribcage invisible for the rest of her life.

"I saw your aunt Monica in the bank this morning," Elaine announced, picking up the party dress from a nearby chair and dropping the pink confection over Leda's head.

Temporarily imprisoned in chiffon, Leda closed her eyes. Elaine was her aunt's age, a grandmother, and a bigger gossip than Monica, if that was possible. Their conversation must have been interesting.

It was. "She told me that Reardon fella was out of jail," Elaine mumbled through a mouthful of pins. "They didn't keep him locked up long enough, if you ask me." She tugged expertly on the net bodice of the dress.

I didn't ask you, Leda thought as the folds of material settled around her legs. Elaine pulled and tucked and adjusted, taking in the seams of the gown. As she did so she kept up a running monologue on the disgraceful return to Yardley of the unwanted convict Kyle Reardon. Leda listened in silence, fascinated by this outpouring of venom against a man Elaine didn't even know.

"No one will give him a job, of course," Elaine concluded with satisfaction. "He'll by panhandling in the streets pretty soon, unless he moves."

"I guess that's the general idea," Leda observed dryly, wincing a little as Elaine stuck her with a pin. "To get him to move."

Elaine glanced at her sharply. "I wouldn't think *you* would want to see him back here," she said tartly.

Leda made a dismissive gesture. "Elaine, I was away when it all happened, and it was a long time ago. I suppose I should hate Reardon, but I really find it difficult to hate anybody."

"Well, you wouldn't say that if you'd been in town at the time. Your poor father. He was a very popular man hereabouts, and Yardley is a small community with a long memory. You can't expect people to forget that all they did was lock that hothead up for a few years and take away his pilot's license. Small price to pay for your father's life, and the lives of the others who died in that accident."

"He can't earn his living without his permit," Leda pointed out. "Don't you think that's going to hurt him?"

"He's trying to get it back," Elaine said huffily, gesturing for Leda to turn around. "He filed in Harrisburg already, I heard."

"How do you know?" Leda asked suspiciously, craning her neck to look over her shoulder.

"Stand still," Elaine barked, lifting the hem of the dress and examining it. "Where are the shoes you wear with this?"

Leda pointed, and Elaine scooped the high-heeled pumps off the floor. Leda stepped into them, and Elaine crouched down, muttering to herself.

"I asked you how you knew so much about Kyle Reardon," Leda repeated holding herself rigid.

"He rented that apartment above Sara Master's garage," Elaine replied. "He gets his mail in the same box she does."

"Sara's been reading his mail!" Leda exclaimed, shocked into motion. The fabric tore out of Elaine's hand.

"Stop jumping around!" Elaine said, exasperated. "You're going to look like a harlequin in this dress if you don't settle down."

"Has Sara Master been reading that man's mail?" Leda asked in a strong voice, ignoring the reprimand.

"Of course not," Elaine answered mildly. "But she sees the return addresses on the envelopes he receives. He's been writing to the FAA division in the state capitol."

Leda felt a flash of sympathy for Reardon. He was the new grist in the rumor mill. To the gossip mongers in town he was a fascinating blackguard with a dark past, and the closest they'd ever get to the villains they saw in the movies.

"Maybe I should tell him to find a new apartment," Leda suggested.

Elaine stared up at her. "Surely you wouldn't speak to him," she said. The sarcasm of Leda's comment was lost on her.

"Somebody should inform him that his landlady's a spy," Leda said in clarification.

"Sara is not a spy. She can't help but notice what goes on right under her nose. She wouldn't have rented to him at all, you know, but she needs the money. Rafe's arthritis has been acting up something terrible. He's got this pain in his lower back and they had to take him to a specialist—"

"I think Sara would be better off minding her own business," Leda interrupted, to forestall a lengthy catalog of Rafe's symptoms. "And so would you."

Elaine rose and glared at her. "You sound like you feel sorry for him," she said accusingly. "The man practically killed your father."

"Nobody killed my father," Leda said, pulling the dress back over her head. "He died of a heart attack."

"After Reardon caused the accident that brought it on," Elaine said, shaking out the dress and replacing it on its hanger. "I trust you haven't forgotten that."

"I haven't forgotten anything," Leda said wearily, tiring of the subject. "Where is that sundress for the picnic scenes?"

Elaine went to get it, throwing Leda a dirty look over her shoulder.

Leda shook her head. If this was a sample of the kind of reception Reardon was getting, he had to be having a jolly time.

During the following week many of Leda's neighbors stopped her to express their outrage at the return of the local pariah, Kyle Reardon. Since Leda had only recently moved back to town herself, they greeted her warmly, expressing delight that she was among them again. Then they took the opportunity to shake their heads and wonder aloud what Reardon was thinking of, to come back to a place where he wasn't welcome. Leda often diverted the subject to her relocation, explaining that since she had taken the job at the playhouse, she'd subletted the apartment she shared with another actress in New York. It made economic sense to live in the duplex and commute to the city when she had to, rather than run back and forth for her performances in New Hope. Her father's friends nodded politely and quickly skipped back to the more interesting topic, the felon in their midst. The endless inquiries exhausted Leda, and she soon learned to cut the conversations short.

In all the talk she never heard one word in Reardon's defense.

And on a couple of occasions she had firsthand experience of the treatment Reardon was receiving from the good citizens of Yardley. One afternoon she was in the pharmacy on South Main Street, standing unobserved behind a high counter, when Reardon walked in and asked for a bottle of iodine and a packet of gauze. He was wearing the same jacket he had worn in the graveyard, and there was a large, angry-looking cut next to his left eye. The result of an altercation? Leda wondered. She watched as the druggist, an old golfing buddy of her father's, treated Reardon with such glacial politeness that the effect was more offensive than the grossest insult would have been. Another time she saw him walking, erect and alone, through a chattering crowd gathering on the walk outside the movie theater. The show had just ended, and she paused on her way to her car from the convenience store across the street to observe the scene. The throng parted as if by magic to let him pass through. The people stared at him in rigid silence until he was almost out of earshot, and then someone made a comment Leda couldn't hear. Reardon heard it, though; she saw him break stride and then recover, his broad shoulders squaring as if in anticipation of a blow. None came, however, and he walked on, never glancing back, as the onlookers snickered nastily, reacting to what had been said.

Leda's expression was thoughtful as she stowed her package in the backseat of her car and started for home. She couldn't help feeling a grudging admiration for Reardon's stoic endurance. He took all the abuse directed at him, subtle or overt, with quiet dignity, as if he expected it and had made up his mind to tolerate it.

The image of him striding purposefully through that hostile assembly, eyes straight ahead, the lights of the theater marquee glinting on his dark hair, haunted her until she wished she could forget it.

About ten days after her accidental meeting with Reardon in the cemetery, Leda received a call from the businessman who had purchased the hangar and airstrip formerly used by her father's company. Matthew Phelps was a newcomer to the area, and when he had inquired about buying the property through Leda's lawyer, she was surprised. It had been listed for years with no show of interest. Airstrips were not exactly in big demand. But he'd offered a fair price, just enough for Leda to satisfy the mortgage against it. The new owner ran a charter company, making supply runs and transporting groups of vacationers to sunny islands. Phelps asked if she would come out to the hangar office and pick up some personal items of her father's that had been overlooked and were still there, ledgers and notebooks and even some clothes. Leda was tempted to tell him to pack the stuff up and give it to charity. She had no wish to relive painful experiences by sorting through belongings she hadn't even known existed. But her innate good manners won out and she told Phelps she would be out that evening, steeling herself for a visit to her father's former milieu, where she would surely hear the echo of happier times. When his wife died, Carter Bradshaw had focused all his energies on his only child, and Leda had spent a lot of time with him at his office. She'd done her homework on his desk and watched television on a small portable set in his anteroom while he took care of business. Once she went away to school she missed the smell of exhaust and engine grease, the heat and bustle of the lab where the technicians tested parts and fuels and lubricants. It would be difficult to go back there now and see it all in the hands of someone else.

The night was cold, threatening more snow, as Leda drove past the long, low industrial buildings that flanked the airfield. The slate-gray structure of the hangar loomed before her as she parked her car and walked through the huge doors toward the office just inside.

The noise of engines was constant, and deafening. Phelps kept a crew working all night, as her father had done, and the men in overalls scurried about, fueling a helicopter and a Piper Cub from a truck nearby. Frigid air rushed in through the open wall, and Leda hurried across the cement floor, intent on reaching the warmth of the business enclosure. She glanced around for Phelps, and stopped dead in her tracks.

Bending over the fuselage of the Piper Cub, absorbed in overhauling the engine, was a very filthy Kyle Reardon.

Two

"Miss Bradshaw?"

Leda started out of her reverie, turning to face the man who addressed her. "Yes?"

He was a middle-aged, freckled redhead with an open, engaging manner. He stuck out his hand. "I'm Jim Kendall, the plant manager here. Matt Phelps asked me to meet you. He's tied up at the moment, but he should be with you shortly. Would you like to sit in the office and wait?"

Leda nodded, glancing once more at Reardon. He worked on, oblivious of her presence. She shook Kendall's hand and followed him past the opaque glass partition that separated the administration area from the hangar.

"I understand your father used to own this place," Kendall said conversationally as she sat down next to a green metal filing cabinet.

"Yes, Mr. Phelps purchased it from the estate."

Kendall helped himself to coffee from a pot on a warmer near the door. Leda shook her head when he asked her if she wanted any, and he added powdered creamer to his drink as he talked.

"Your father was a real popular guy around here," Kendall said. "I ran into some trouble with a few of the workers when I hired that Reardon fella, the one who got into the scrape with that test. He had a rough couple of days when he started, but he's settling in now. I believe in giving a guy a second chance, and he's a crack mechanic. It's quite a comedown for him too, working as a grease monkey, but he's taking it like a trouper."

Leda eyed Kendall nervously, wondering why he was telling her all this.

"I saw you watching him when I came up to you," Kendall explained reading her expression. "I thought I'd better clear it up, in case there were any hard feelings."

"Mr. Reardon has paid his debt to society. Isn't that the phrase." Leda replied stiffly. "You have the right to employ anybody you please."

Kendall's brow furrowed. He obviously wasn't sure what to make of her comment. He looked up at the clock on the wall and tossed his empty cup into the trash.

"Miss Bradshaw, I have to go. Would you mind if I left you alone for a little while? I'm sure Matt will be out directly."

"Go ahead," Leda said, relieved that the man was leaving. She was afraid she was in for further discussion of Reardon if he stayed. After Kendall was gone, she sat waiting for about ten minutes, and then, bored with the inactivity, got up to have a look around. Phelps was obviously delayed, and she might as well amuse herself until he showed up.

She couldn't quite admit that she wanted another look at Reardon.

Once back out on the floor, Leda searched for him, trying to be as unobtrusive as possible. He wasn't difficult to find. Though attired like the others in nondescript overalls, he stood a head taller than most of the men, and his vivid coloring drew her eye. The Piper Cub was gone, and he was now working on a much larger Beechcraft. The prospective passengers stood nearby, apparently a charter group en route to a Caribbean vacation. They had started the holiday early with some liquid cheer. Several of the men were already loudly, thoroughly drunk.

It wasn't long before Leda realized that she had walked into the middle of a tense situation. The expression on Reardon's face was set, his mouth hard, and tendons stood out in his powerful arms as he tightened a bolt on the metal frame of the plane.

"You musta gotten pretty lonely up there," one of the travelers called, nudging the man next to him. "I hear some funny stuff goes on in the lockup when a man gets lonely enough."

The group cracked up laughing, as if this were the most hilarious bon mot that had ever been uttered. Reardon went on working, pretending to be oblivious, but his posture indicated that he was aware of every syllable.

"What's it like to be a jailbird?" the first man's companion added. "What do you miss, the decor, the company, the food?"

Reardon looked up, and his eyes were murderous. Leda shrank back against the wall, trying to be invisible, hoping that she could get back behind the partition before she was noticed. These drunken bullies had heard Reardon's story from somewhere and were having some malicious fun by taunting him about his past. She began to move silently sideways, edging back toward the office.

But it was too late. The first loudmouth caught sight of her and pointed, caroling, "Boy, you been locked up so long, you wouldn't know what to do with a woman like that if you got near one."

Reardon's head turned in the direction of the pointing finger, and his silvery eyes met Leda's alarmed gaze. They widened as he recognized her, and Leda's heart sank. There would be no avoiding a confrontation now; this giggling bunch of overstimulated sots would find the opportunity too good to miss.

Reardon continued to look at her, his attention shifting from his antagonists to the object of their commentary. Leda held her breath, dreading what might happen next. He carefully put aside the wrench he'd been holding, never taking his eyes from hers.

"Out of practice, aren't ya?" a third member of the audience chimed in, adding his wit to that previously displayed. "Ya wouldn't know where to begin with her, would ya?"

A deep flush was creeping up the back of Reardon's neck. He was being pushed to the edge. Those engaging in the catcalling didn't know who Leda was, or the history between Reardon and her father, but she did, and she could see that Reardon was approaching the boiling point. A little muscle in his clenched jaw

was jumping wildly. He might have been able to en-
dure the jeering, he had done it before, but his em-
barrassment and humiliation in front of Leda were too
much. She watched as his fingers curled and relaxed,
saw the checked, coiled spring power of his legs as he
struggled to master his feelings. For the first time she
got a sense of the temper and the stubborn will that
had precipitated his original trouble. Monica was
right. Prison hadn't changed him. He had merely
learned some controls on his behavior, controls that
were about to snap with the report of a pistol shot.

Leda swallowed, wondering what to do. She had to
take action. If she didn't step in to defuse this ticking
bomb, the revelers would get a lot more than they had
bargained for. If they weren't so far gone they would
be able to see that for themselves, Leda thought, her
heart going out to Reardon. This personal attack on
him was so unfair. She could guess from her own ob-
servation how hard he had tried to put the pieces of his
shattered life back together and erase the stigma of his
past. But to be subjected to this, in front of a witness
about whom he was bound to be sensitive, was too
much. Leda had simulated rage often enough in her
profession to recognize an incipient outburst of the
real thing. Reardon was going to take the place apart.

She acted without conscious thought, almost without volition. She knew only one thing: if Reardon vi-
olated his parole by getting into a brawl on the job, he
would most likely wind up back in prison.

Leda walked across the floor to the point where
Reardon was standing next to the plane. All eyes
moved to her as she took center stage, deliberately
calling attention to herself as she had earlier tried to
avoid it.

Reardon stared at her in disbelief as she approached him, clearly wondering what this madwoman was doing. Leda stopped in front of him, her eyes barely on a level with his collarbone. The onlookers were silent as she placed her hands on his shoulders.

He flinched slightly, glancing down at himself, his dirty clothes, his grimy hands. But she tightened her grip, and he stood still, his unusual eyes darkening with some emotion as they looked into hers.

I hope this works, Leda prayed, and I hope he doesn't misinterpret what I'm doing. He waited, as did everyone else, for her next move.

"There's no problem if he doesn't know where to begin with me," she announced, feigning a playfulness she didn't feel. "I know where to begin with him." She stood on tiptoe and kissed him.

Reardon remained motionless for a timeless instant, and then Leda felt the total response of his body in a single fluid movement. His lips opened, covering hers, taking the initiative masterfully, and his arms enclosed her in a muscular grip, binding her to him. One large hand moved up her spine, caressing her back, and then sank into her hair. He held her steady, his fingers massaging her nape as his mouth took hers with such hunger, such total abandon, that Leda clung to him, reeling. Reardon made a sound, half sigh, half groan, and pulled her even tighter, fusing her hips to his. Leda gasped against his lips as she felt his arousal. She was bathed in sensation: the texture of his skin, the lean strength of his limbs, the surprising softness of his mouth. His scent surrounded her, an intoxicating blend of acrid sweat and diesel fuel, astringent shampoo and the underlying notes of cedar soap and the starch of his once clean coveralls. Her fingers slid luxuriously into the wealth of hair at the back of his head as she responded to him eagerly, powerless to resist. She forgot their audience, and everything else.

The group looked on in dumb fascination, hushed, riveted by the human drama taking place before their very eyes. Those most vocal in tormenting Reardon finally looked away, embarrassed because the only thing they had achieved was not his humiliation, but a demonstration of his virility. He had unwittingly turned the tables on them by making this desirable woman want him so quickly, and so much, that she had completely lost track of her surroundings. The other workmen watched also, drawn by the power of the scene and the absorption of the two participants in each other. It didn't take a genius to see that they weren't faking it; they were so lost in the experience that they might just as well have been alone.

A bell clanged throughout the hangar, shattering the tableau, signaling the start of the lunch hour for the 4-12 shift. Leda tensed in Reardon's arms, rudely awakened from her dreamlike detachment, and pulled away from him. He brought her back to him, his eyes still closed, his lips parted to take hers again, and it required every ounce of her willpower to sever the connection between them and resist his unspoken invitation. She took a step back, and his eyes opened. His gaze seared hers, his gray eyes transformed from cold platinum to molten steel. Oh, my God, Leda thought wildly as they beckoned her back to his embrace, what have I done?

They stared at each other as the Phelps employees moved toward the cafeteria and the members of the charter group shuffled nervously in the background and struck up a conversation among themselves. Leda heard the high-pitched whine of a rotor behind them, and realized that the noise had continued during the whole encounter, but she hadn't heard it. It was as if she had been suspended in a vacuum with Reardon, heedless of mundane concerns like sound and temperature. She shivered as she noticed once more that she was cold. Had she been unaware of it, or had Reardon kept her warm?

"Are you all right?" Reardon asked her in an undertone the others couldn't hear. His normally deep voice was hoarse.

Leda nodded, unable to speak. She trembled violently and, annoyed at her body's betrayal, wrapped her arms around her torso.

"You're cold," Reardon said. He moved swiftly to the cabin of the plane he'd been servicing and produced the leather jacket she'd seen him wearing. He returned and extended it to her.

"Put this on," he said gruffly.

Leda shook her head.

"Take it," he commanded. "You're shivering."

Leda didn't object as he draped it around her shoulders. The lining inside was thick, wooly alpaca, and she snuggled into it gratefully.

"My coat is back in the office," she finally said, finding her voice. "I'll leave this there when I go."

He didn't answer, merely gazed down at her, his breathing visible in the rise and fall of his deep chest. He wanted to say more, so much in fact, but words failed him.

"I have to meet Mr. Phelps," Leda said lamely. It sounded inane to her own ears.

Reardon's eyes left her and he scanned the little band of vacationers, unsure of what to do with themselves now that the crises they had provoked was over. His lip curled derisively.

"They wanted a show," he said grimly. "They got one."

"I'm sorry about what they said," Leda replied softly. "People can be very cruel sometimes, and drink often brings out the worst in them."

He brought his hand up and touched her cheek. "I know why you did that," he said quietly. "Thanks."

Before she could answer he turned away and strode off toward the labs at the back of the hangar, passing the charter group on his way. He didn't even look at them.

Leda turned her back on the travelers and returned to the office, avoiding the curious glances of people in the hangar who had witnessed what happened with her and Reardon. When she got back to the office she sat down and tried to recover her equilibrium. She was still wearing Reardon's jacket.

She felt different, changed, as if she had suddenly realized, in the space of a few minutes, a basic truth about herself that had always lain dormant, just below the surface of her consciousness. She had lived so long in the world of rational behavior that the burst of passion she'd just experienced was like the harsh beam of a searchlight trained on her psyche, forcing her to face her innermost desires. She had saved her ardor for the stage, keeping her relationships with men friendly and uninvolved. If a man pressed for more, she politely but firmly sent him packing. It took long years and hard work to get established in the theatrical world, and she had no time for demanding suitors who might distract her from the goals she sought. But one brief interlude in Kyle Reardon's arms had changed all that. Leda stared at a calendar on the wall, not seeing it, shell-shocked and shaking with the force of emotions that threatened to alter the balance of her world forever.

That's it, she thought. That's why women give up everything and follow a man, that's why they'll do anything to be with him and not care about the rest. She had read about the power of such attraction, seen it portrayed in films, and even acted it out herself in the theater. But she had never experienced it personally until this night. And with the last man on earth she would have chosen, the betrayer of her father's trust.

The door opened behind her and Matthew Phelps walked through it. You're too late, Leda thought dryly, too late to save me. This lady is already lost.

"I'm so sorry," Phelps began. "I know you've been waiting awhile. I hope you didn't get too bored." He sat down across from her.

Leda restrained herself from laughing at that, but her smile was broad.

"Don't worry about it," she said. "Jim Kendall explained that you were going to be held up."

"These meetings," he signed, rolling his eyes. "They always go on longer than anybody thinks they will." He paused and examined Leda closely his eyes narrowing.

"Are you okay, Miss Bradshaw?" he asked, his tone concerned. "You're very pale, and you look like you're cold."

"I'm fine," Leda stated with far more conviction than she felt. "I just went into the hangar without my coat, and got chilled."

"I see one of the men gave you his jacket," Phelps said. His blue eyes were grave. He knew whose jacket it was.

"Yes," Leda replied evenly. "Kyle Reardon."

Phelps took a packet of cigarettes from his breast pocket, removing one and tapping it on the cover of the box. "Did you know he was working here?"

"Not until this evening."

He nodded his head. "Perhaps I should have told you before you came out tonight." He struck a match, watching her.

Leda shrugged. "There was no reason for you to do that. Kendall explained that Reardon is a good mechanic, and deserves a second chance."

"I'm glad you see it that way," Phelps said, lighting his cigarette and inhaling deeply. "Shall we go inside and get your father's things?"

Leda nodded, standing with him and following in his path. He led her toward the back of the office, to the corridor that served the inner storage rooms.

She couldn't help thinking that Phelps would interpret this conversation in a different light when he heard, as he surely would, what had happened to Leda while he was gone.

In the days that followed Leda's visit to the Phelps hangar, she tried to tell herself that she had exaggerated the impact of the incident with Reardon. She was a championship rationalizer, and had talked herself out of any number of potential relationships in the past. She was working very hard at doing it again.

But this time it wasn't working. Reardon invaded her life, hovering in the background, always on her mind or just at the edge of it, defeating her best efforts to cast him into oblivion. But Leda didn't give up. She had resisted the lure of other men in the past, and she could do it once more. Maybe Reardon was a stronger presence than the others, but that didn't mean she had to revert to schoolgirl daydreams and speculation about where he was and what he was doing. With a little more effort, she would be able to dismiss him too.

She had no way of knowing how wrong she was.

Three

Reardon let himself into his empty apartment and tossed his keys onto a shelf. He'd just bought the car they operated, and it was a clunker. He couldn't afford anything better at the moment, however, and he had great faith in his ability to fix all types of machinery. He smiled to himself bitterly. The car should prove to be the ultimate challenge to his abilities.

He glanced around at the two bare rooms, sparsely furnished with the essentials that he had managed to assemble from secondhand shops and rummage sales. He thought briefly of the luxurious condominium he had owned before his trial, and which had been sold, along with the Porsche and the blue chip stocks, to pay for his legal representation. All to no avail. He had wound up in prison anyway. He sighed, his eyes drawn to the one feature of the cheerless dwelling that served to brighten his spirits. A marvelous stone fireplace, with the original oak mantel, took up almost all the space along one exterior wall. It had been used for drying purposes when the area above the garage was a storeroom, and he had gotten Mrs. Master's permission to refurbish it and use it. He had stripped the wood of the mantel down to the grain, and then stained it, following that with a clear lacquer. He found that manual labor occupied his free time and made him tired enough to sleep at night. Once the fireplace was in shape, he kept logs burning in it almost constantly when he was home. If a person could actually call such a place home.

Reardon shrugged out of his jacket, and his fingers lingered on the collar as he moved to put it down. She wore this, he thought, and then tossed it furiously aside.

That Bradshaw girl. She kept turning up, making it impossible for him to forget her, distracting him from his singular purpose in returning to Yardley. No matter how attractive he found her, she was Carter Bradshaw's daughter, and sure to hate him. He mustn't lose sight of that fact.

Other things remained in his mind instead. The way she had looked when she touched his arm at her father's grave, tentative, searching, alive with curiosity. The way she had come to his aid at the Phelps hangar, the impulse of kindness that had turned into the kiss he could still taste, still feel. The color of her eyes, the softness of her hair...Reardon pressed his lips together, refusing to continue the train of thought. He had to stop thinking about her. It was driving him crazy.

He didn't need this. He didn't need to wonder about her or dream about her, which he did almost every night. The dreams were the worst. They weren't bad dreams. He was used to those; he'd had nightmares constantly ever since he went to jail. The dreams concerning Leda were different, tantalizing excursions into erotica from which he awoke tormented, his muscles in knots, his body bathed in sweat that soaked the sheets twisted around his limbs like coiled snakes. Sleep was impossible after such episodes. He would often lie awake until it was time to get up, reliving the fantasy in his mind.

He wanted to believe that such a reaction was normal for a man in his situation. Leda Bradshaw was the only woman he had touched in four years, the only female who had held him, kissed him, in a very long time. It was only natural for him to respond to that, wasn't it? Surely his obsession with her was nothing more than the reaction of a starved man to his first sight, and taste, of food.

But he wasn't able to convince himself completely. He was attractive to women, he knew that. Since his release from prison he had discovered that this remained unchanged; he'd had other chances, with other ladies, and had turned them down.

He'd turned them down because he wanted Leda Bradshaw.

Leda shut the door of her dressing room and wedged the top of a chair under the knob to block it. She was dodging Chip Caswell, as usual, and he had a tendency to barge in unannounced, probably hoping to catch her in a state of undress. She sat in front of her lighted mirror and wondered what she was going to do about her leading man.

Chip was a veteran thespian in his thirties, with an extensive career in stock and a two-year stint on a syndicated series for a cable station to his credit. This, plus several guest spots on nighttime television, had long ago convinced him that he was in league with Laurence Olivier. What he was doing playing opposite Leda in the outback of eastern Pennsylvania was anybody's guess, but Leda suspected that it had something to do with his reputation for easy living and hard drinking. He had probably become too unreliable to sell to the networks, as evidenced by his late appearances for morning rehearsals, bleary eyed and hung over to the point of incoherence. So far his looks hadn't suffered much, so he was still employable, and he enjoyed his work very much, strutting around in designer jeans, posing like a male model. Leda thought he should have been one. His all-American-boy appeal was a strong selling point, and he was handsome if you liked the type.

Leda didn't like the type. His goal during this theatrical engagement was to get her into bed, and he spent most of his time attempting to charm Leda out of her socks. And other items of clothing. The charm was beginning to wear a little thin in the face of her total unresponsiveness, but Chip was a patient man. He simply couldn't believe she meant what she said. He was certain she would cave in eventually. And given his apparent track record, his conceit was justified.

Leda looked up at a knock on the door.

"Who is it?" she called, wincing. If it was Chip, nothing short of a death announcement would make him go away.

"Your roommate," a woman's voice answered.

Leda got up to remove the chair. It was Anna Fleming, the actress who played Leda's mother in the show. She shared the dressing room. Anna raised her brows as she entered and saw Leda replacing the chair against the wall.

"Expecting company?" she asked.

"You might say that."

"Young Lochinvar?" Anna asked, grinning. She found Chip's pursuit of Leda an endless source of amusement.

"Very funny," Leda said darkly.

"You could always hire a bodyguard. Honestly, sweetie, I don't understand you. Haven't you seen all those panting young things asking Chip for his autograph after every performance? Just think what they would do with the opportunity you're passing up."

"They can have him," Leda said, sitting down again and opening up a new package of sponges to apply her makeup. "They can all read his press clippings together."

"Have you seen my powder?" Anna asked, shifting things on her side of the room. She sat on the floor and unzipped a vinyl carryall, dumping its contents on the tile.

"Are you looking for that stuff again?" Leda asked. "Can't you keep track of it?"

"If that tightwad Gary would get me a wig, I wouldn't have this problem," Anna muttered, picking up an emery board and starting to file her nails. "I look ridiculous with that junk on my head anyway."

Leda smiled in silent agreement. Anna was referring to a decision made by Gary Randall, their director, who was notorious for pinching pennies. Anna was in her thirties, playing an older woman who was

the mother of a girl in her twenties. Gary's solution to
the problem of aging Anna was to liberally dust her
dark hair with talcum powder, instead of purchasing
the gray wig Anna wanted. Leda and Anna privately
thought that this tactic made Anna look like a thirty-
two-year-old woman with a head full of dusting powder; it didn't help that Anna gave off a small scented
cloud anytime somebody touched her. Cast and crew
alike referred to her as "The Dust Bowl."

Anna had left the door ajar when she entered, and
a stagehand came in with a plastic bag draped over his
shoulder.

"Elaine dropped these costumes off earlier," he said
to Leda. He hung the bag on a coatrack fixed to the
wall. "She told me to say you should let her know if
the alterations are okay."

"Too bad for me if they aren't," Leda said after the
boy left. "I'll be wearing those dresses in forty
minutes."

"Full house tonight," Anna commented, now
plugging in her electric rollers. "Gary informed me on
my way in. Let's hope Peter doesn't fall into the orchestra pit."

Peter Jenkins played the local merchant who married the old maid schoolteacher in the play. Peter was
a former matinee idol in the B pictures of the forties,
down on his luck now and reduced to playing sup-
porting roles whenever he could get the work. The
reason for his downfall was obvious. Although Chip
often *looked* the worse for wear, he was always sober
for performances, while Peter was usually dead drunk.

"Do you think Gary will fire him?" Leda asked. It
amazed her that Peter had lasted this long. Gary didn't
tolerate much nonsense.

"Nah," Anna replied. "Didn't you know? Gary's dad and Peter were friends in the old days. Peter got the old man his first job or something. Gary will carry him for the full run."

Leda thought that over. Gary's late father had been a big name in Hollywood, before the blacklisting of the fifties had ended his career. Gary had his faults, but he was very loyal.

"Here it is," Anna said triumphantly, extracting a tin of powder from a hatbox on the radiator. "I forgot I put it in there."

Leda turned to look at what she was doing. "Anna, don't put that cardboard box on the radiator. You know we can't control the heat in that old thing. One of these days we're both going to go up in smoke."

"It's a wonder this whole place hasn't burned down long before this," Anna replied irritably. "When was it built, during the Revolution? What a firetrap. And whoever heard of doing *Picnic* in December anyway? We should be putting on *A Christmas Carol* or *The Winter's Tale*."

Leda didn't answer, aware of the reason for Anna's discontent. She'd recently gone down to the wire for the role of Nora in a PBS revival of *A Doll's House,* and lost out at the last minute to a mysterious late arrival. Anna subsequently discovered that the victor was the producer's new girlfriend.

Leda sighed. Everybody knew that sort of thing went on in this business, but it still hurt when it happened to you.

Finished with her foundation, Leda picked up the tube of bloodred lipstick she used to transform herself into Madge Owens.

It was enough to make an actress retire from the stage and become a librarian.

Several hours later Leda was back home, sipping a glass of wine and trying to recover from an unmitigated disaster.

Everything had gone wrong during that evening's performance. The crew missed their cues, the actors forgot their lines, and the prop man dropped a bucket backstage when Anna was making her entrance. During Chip's big dramatic speech, which demanded the breathless attention of the audience, a cat leaped from the balcony onto the stage. The accompanist was a substitute, called in at the eleventh hour when the regular pianist took ill, and the new person brought his own sheet music, unfamiliar to Chip and Leda. The resulting dance scene, meant to be slow and seductive, looked more like a beer barrel polka.

Leda took another swallow, closing her eyes. Things had gone on in that vein all night, mistake after mishap, until by the final curtain Leda was seriously considering suicide. The bewildered audience had been gracious about the debacle, but that didn't make the crestfallen company feel any better. Gary had given them all a pep talk afterward, which fell on deaf ears. Leda could only remember one performance worse than this, a college production of *A Midsummer Night's Dream*, in which she had played Titania. On that occasion Puck had fallen out of the plastic tree set up on stage for his revels, and broken his leg. Leda's recollection of the rest of that evening was mercifully blurred, but the experience was sufficient to drive her to the registrar's office the next morning, intent on changing her major from drama to anything else. The head of the department had talked her out of it when she brought him the drop forms for his signature. Up until now, she'd been glad he did. But she was discouraged once again. There were few things worse than making a fool out of yourself in front of a houseful of people expecting to be entertained.

Leda heard footsteps on the porch she shared with Claire, and realized that the other woman was coming home. The feet paused in mid-stride and switched direction. Leda got up as Claire rapped sharply on the glass pane set in her door.

"Leda, are you in there?" Claire called.

Leda opened her door and stepped aside to let Claire pass. Claire took in the bottle on the end table and glanced at Leda with concern. Leda rarely drank.

"What happened?" she said, taking off her coat and scarf and sitting down.

"What didn't happen?" Leda responded drearily.

"Bad show?"

"You could say that. The performance we gave tonight would have been more appropriate for the Marx Brothers or the Keystone Cops."

"Tell me," Claire said, removing her boots.

Leda did, concluding with, "And to top it all off, Chip stepped on my dress in the third act and ripped out the hem Elaine put in, and I was tripping all over it for the rest of the scene. I'm lucky I didn't try to walk away while he was standing on it, or I would have been revealed to the audience in the pristine glory of my strapless slip. And the rope almost came loose from the ceiling when I sat in the swing. I keep telling the grip about it; one of these nights I'm going to get pitched right into the first row."

Claire sighed. "And I thought finger painting with first graders was exciting."

Leda snorted. "I'd rather be doing that than head-lining with amateur night in Dixie."

"Just think of the experience you're getting," Claire said comfortingly, rubbing her toes. "You'll look back on all this fondly when you're accepting your Oscar."

"Claire, the way I feel right now, I have a better chance of colonizing Mars than I have of winning an Academy Award."

Claire got up and reached for the ashtray on the piano. She sat back in her chair and curled her legs underneath her, taking her cigarettes out of her purse.

"Are you going to tell me about it?" she asked quietly.

"I just did."

"No, I mean the real reason you've been in such a funk lately. You've turned down two invitations to go shopping, one lunch, and a free ticket to a Broadway show. Either my company has begun to pall, or you are preoccupied to the point of catatonia. You seem to spend most of your free time holed up in here, staring at the walls. What's going on?"

Leda didn't answer.

"It's him, isn't it? That Reardon guy."

Leda's eyes flashed to her face.

"I thought so," Claire said, nodding. "What's up?" She lit a cigarette, shaking out the match and dropping it into the ashtray. She inhaled deeply, watching Leda closely.

Leda shrugged. "I saw him again the other night, when I went out to the Phelps hangar to pick up my father's stuff."

"You mean after you ran into him at the cemetery."

"Right," Leda said shortly.

"And?" Claire inquired, raising her brows.

Leda made a dismissive gesture. "Claire, I should be paying you by the hour. I'm sure you have better things to do than listen to my problems."

Claire shook her head, exhaling a stream of smoke. "Nice try, kiddo. You can't evade me that easily. Tell Mother all about it."

Leda recounted what had happened at the hangar. Silence reigned when she finished, as Claire smoked thoughtfully, considering what had been said.

"Well?" Leda prompted her.

Claire's eyes widened. "All I can say is, from your reaction since it happened, that must have been some kiss."

Leda stood abruptly, pacing. "Claire, you're not helping me. I can't seem to put him out of my mind. What's going on?"

Claire dragged deeply on the stub she held, then crushed it out. "Offhand, I'd say you're hung up on this guy."

Leda whirled to face her. "Don't be ridiculous. I've only seen him twice."

Claire nodded. "And you think it can't happen like that? I've seen you supposedly bloodless types before when you get the call. You fall hard, and fast, and forever. This guy's already got you talking to yourself and walking into furniture. Don't kid yourself, Leda, you've got it bad."

"This can't be happening," Leda said, pushing back her hair. "I'm not ready for this."

Claire rubbed the bridge of her nose in exasperation. "Did you really think you could put it all on a timetable, a career alone for so many years, and then when you decide, when things are in order, you'd meet a nice guy, get married, have kids, tra la la?''

"I guess I did," Leda replied glumly, sitting again and putting her chin in her hand.

Claire shook her finger at Leda. "I always said you're a lot more naive than you look. For example, with that face and figure, who would believe that you've only had one lover in your entire twenty-five years of life?"

"Why don't you put it on the six o'clock news, Claire?" Leda said sarcastically.

"Winfield Scott," Claire went on airily, ignoring her. "He's the reason for your aloofness with men. You just won't admit it."

Leda looked away, not replying. Claire had struck a nerve. Win Scott had been the director of the first production Leda acted in after her graduation from college. He'd seduced Leda, who thought herself in love, and then moved on to the next conquest when the run ended. It had left Leda with a bad impression of relationships, and it had taken her a long time to get over it. She'd avoided such entanglements ever since.

"It's more than just the timing, isn't it?" Claire asked, breaking into her thoughts.

Leda smiled derisively. "Come on, Claire. The choice could hardly be worse. You know what happened in the past, you know the whole history between Reardon and my father. If I scoured the earth I couldn't find a less suitable—"

"Mate?" Claire suggested innocently, and Leda threw her a dirty look.

"Don't make faces at me," Claire said defensively. "I mean, what are we talking about here? I don't think you want to play pinochle with him, after all."

"I don't want to do anything with him," Leda said despairingly.

"Yes, you do," Claire replied. "And I know why. I've seen him." She favored Leda with a mischievous grin.

Leda looked at her. "You didn't tell me that."

"You didn't give me a chance. As I recall, since I arrived you've done all the talking," Claire said indignantly.

"Where did you see him?"

"In town, at the post office. Betty Parsons pointed him out to me."

Betty Parsons was the postmistress, the third part of the triumvirate that included Leda's aunt Monica and Elaine. Sara Master, Reardon's landlady, was part of the hoi polloi that served under these three, coddling favor with little tidbits of gossip but never actually rising to the level of the autocracy. Sara's stock must have jumped dramatically with Reardon's arrival, Leda thought dryly.

"Very attractive," Claire pronounced sagely. "Great body. Nice eyes too. Blue, aren't they?"

"Gray," Leda corrected, and Claire laughed.

"All right, so I noticed," Leda admitted, flushing faintly.

"Does he know who you are?" Claire asked, sobering.

Leda nodded slowly. "Yes, I'm sure he does, though he's never actually said so."

"Not much chance for him to," Claire observed practically. "You've only been with him a couple of times, briefly."

"That's what frightens me," Leda said seriously. "To be this affected by him, after such limited contact...well, it has me rattled."

The telephone rang.

"Be still, my heart," Claire hissed.

Leda got up to answer it. "Relax, Claire. It's probably the plumber calling to arrange a time to fix my sink."

"Not at eleven-thirty, it isn't," Claire said, glancing at her watch.

It wasn't the plumber, but it wasn't Reardon either. It was Monica, in a snit.

"I heard about that little performance you put on at the Phelps place the other night," Monica announced without preliminary. "Leda Bradshaw, what on earth is the matter with you?"

"Hello, Monica," Leda answered calmly, loud enough for Claire to hear. "Isn't it a little late for you to be calling?"

"I called the moment I heard about it," Monica replied huffily. "Have you taken complete leave of your senses? The whole town is buzzing."

"Who's the whole town, Monica? You and Elaine and that gossipy group of nitpickers you pal around with?"

"There's no need to be sharp with me, young lady. I'm only looking out for your welfare. Think of your reputation, think of your poor father and what that man did to him. I can't believe you would behave this way."

"I don't expect you to understand this, Monica," Leda said wearily, "but I was trying to stop a fight. And I did. That's all there is to it."

"All there is to it!" Monica shrieked. "You throw yourself at the man who ruined your father in front of a room full of staring people and *that's* your explanation?"

Leda held the phone away from her ear and crossed her eyes at Claire. Then she put the receiver back again.

"Word certainly gets around," Leda said bitterly to her aunt. "There weren't that many people there."

"Enough, apparently," Monica said unhappily. "Leda, I don't know how you can be so calm about this. I'm mortified."

"Don't be. You didn't kiss him, I did."

There was a shocked silence from the other end of the line. Leda took advantage of Monica's momentary lapse to end the conversation.

"Monica, I have to go. Claire's here and it's rude to leave her sitting alone while I talk to you. Don't worry about this now. It's over and the gossip will die down. It always does. Good-bye."

"Wait a minute!" Monica protested. "I'm not finished with you."

"Yes you are," Leda said firmly and hung up the phone.

"She was upset," Claire said flatly.

"She certainly was."

"I could guess the reason from your end of the conversation," Claire said. "Well, you can hardly blame her. She sat all through Reardon's trial and saw him convicted. Now she thinks you're making a fool of yourself over an ex-convict whose criminal activities drove your father to his death."

"Is that what you think too?" Leda asked miserably.

Claire shrugged. "I don't know what to think," she replied candidly. "I wasn't around when it all happened. I don't have the same prejudices your aunt does. I can easily see where you would find Reardon compelling, even irresistible, but it might be wise to bear in mind that a jury found him guilty. You may not want to believe that he was responsible for those deaths, but twelve of his peers, who listened to a great deal of evidence, did."

"I know," Leda whispered. "I can't tell you how that preys on my mind."

"I can imagine," Claire said sympathetically. She shifted in her seat. "What are you going to do about your aunt?"

Leda shrugged. "Nothing," she said. "You heard what I said to her. If she insists on dramatizing that incident any further, it's her own fault."

"But we both know there is a real reason for her to be concerned," Claire said quietly.

Leda closed her eyes. "Can we change the subject?"

Claire stood and reached for a notebook she'd brought in with her. "By all means. Help me pick a Christmas project for my elementary classes. What will it be, papier-mâché angels or tinsel ornaments?"

"Oh, papier-mâcheé," Leda answered, smiling. "Kids love to make a mess with it."

"My sentiments exactly," Claire said briskly. "The bigger the mess, the better the time they have." She opened her notebook and gestured for Leda to take a look.

Leda bent over the diagrams obediently, but her mind was on what Claire had said about Reardon. Twelve reasonable people had thought him guilty. Why didn't she?

Two nights later Leda found herself taking a second curtain call, along with the rest of the company, from a packed house. Gary had spoken to the whole cast and crew about this performance, the first since the nightmarish fiasco that Leda had recounted to Claire. The director had boosted everyone's confidence enough to give the show another try, and this time everything worked. The mood was jubilant as the curtain rose again. Leda joined hands with the rest of the principals in a straight line to take a synchronized bow. As she raised her head and looked out at the audience, visible now with the house lights up, she froze.

Kyle Reardon was in the middle of the front row.

Leda moved woodenly, clapping as the bit players took their bow. She watched as he stood with him arms folded, not applauding like the others, but staring intently up at the stage. She couldn't tell if he was looking directly at her.

Leda knew instinctively that his presence was no coincidence. He had found out what she did for a living and had come to see her. She saw him turn while the others were still clapping and make his way toward the aisle. She realized with alarm that he had no intention of making himself known to her and was on his way out.

When the curtain came down, she bolted. Chip called after her to wait, that it was going up again, but she ran on, down the backstage stairs, through the green room, and out into the departing audience. Oblivious of the stares and whispers of the theatergoers who recognized the performer who'd been onstage only moments before, Leda threaded through the milling crowd into the lobby. She spotted Reardon going through the door, and knew that if she didn't attract his attention she would be too late. Still in costume and makeup, she stood on tiptoe and called his name.

"Kyle," she called, projecting her voice as if she were trying to reach the third balcony.

He heard it and stopped. He turned, and his gray eyes met hers over the heads of the people in between as if they weren't there.

He knew instantly who had called him.

Leda raised her hand in greeting, her heart pounding. Reardon held her gaze for a long moment, and Leda wondered if he would turn away and leave.

Then he began to push his way through the crowd toward her. She moved forward too, as best she could, and met in the middle of the jostling throng.

"Hello," she said breathlessly. "I saw you in the audience and came after you. Did you enjoy the play?"

"Yes," he said quietly. "I thought you were very good."

"Would you like to come inside and wait while I change?" Leda asked him, wondering where she got the nerve. "We could go for a drink, there's a place just across the street where the cast drops in after the show."

He didn't answer right away, and Leda's heart sank. I *am* making a fool of myself, she thought wretchedly. Maybe Monica wasn't so wrong.

Then he spoke, and Leda knew the reason for his hesitation.

"Do you know who I am?" he asked, his gaze locked with hers, his mouth grave. He seemed to be holding his breath in anticipation of her response.

"Yes," she said simply. "I know."

"And you still want to go with me?" he asked. His voice was husky, laden with an emotion she couldn't name.

"I asked you, didn't I?"

He extended his hand. "Show me where to go."

Leda took his hand, her fingers lost in his big palm, and led him back to the dressing rooms.

Four

Leda brought Reardon backstage, showing him the way through the warren of partitions and storage areas to the dressing room she shared with Anna. Leda was relieved to see that her roommate wasn't there.

"I'll just be a minute," Leda said to Reardon anxiously, half afraid that he might leave.

He nodded, lounging against the wall and shoving his hands into his pockets. "Take your time." When she remained standing there, looking at him, he added quietly, "Go on. I'll wait."

Leda hurried inside, shutting the door and running to the middle of the room. She didn't know what to do first. Makeup, that was it. She had to remove her makeup. She dashed to her vanity table and reached for the jar of cold cream.

A few minutes later the door opened and Anna came through it. Her expression was awed.

"*Who* is that gorgeous creature out in the hall?" she demanded, jerking her thumb in the direction of the corridor.

"Kyle Reardon," Leda said shortly. Anna was from Chicago, and the name would mean nothing to her.

"You brought him back here?" Anna asked.

"Yes." Leda stepped out of Madge Owens's party dress and headed for the stall shower Gary had rigged in a corner. It was inadequate, with a curtain like a sheet of plastic wrap and a thin stream of lukewarm water, but a decided improvement over banging down the door of the bathroom at the end of the hall.

Anna clapped her hands together. "For me? I know! He's my Christmas present. Leda, you shouldn't have."

"Give me a break, Anna," Leda replied, stripping off her underwear and standing under the tepid dribble. "I'm trying to get out of here in a rush." She soaped her body efficiently.

"I'll bet," Anna said wisely, watching as Leda held her hair up to keep it dry as she rinsed off. "Now I know why you haven't been giving poor Chip Caswell the time of day. Neither would I if I had somebody like that guy outside hanging around at the stage door."

Leda dried herself with her terry bathrobe and reached for her skirt. "Will you hand me that blouse?" she said to Anna, gesturing to the pile of her clothes on a chair. "I hope it isn't too crushed. Oh, why didn't I wear something decent tonight? At every crisis of my life I invariably look like an unmade bed."

"Is this a crisis?" Anna said eagerly, looking interested.

"Forget I said that," Leda responded quickly. "Poor choice of words." She dressed in seconds, snagging her thumbnail on her nylons and muttering under her breath.

"Who is this guy?" Anna asked suspiciously. "You're awfully worked up about his visit."

"Somebody I just met the other day," Leda replied, truthfully enough. "He came to see the show tonight."

"You mean he came to see *you*," Anna corrected her.

"I suppose so," Leda hedged, not even sure why she was trying to keep Anna in the dark about it.

"If not, what's he doing holding up the wall outside this room? I don't think he came to see Peter staggering in and out of the wings, do you? Or Chip doing his Richard Gere imitation?"

"All right," Leda said, trying, and failing to apply lip gloss and eyeliner at the same time. She put down the lip gloss and concentrated on her eyes. "I saw him in the audience and asked him to wait for me."

Anna sighed. "When I look out at the audience all I see are my relatives and the members of my mother's bridge club. Plus a sea of strangers who bear no resemblance to your sexy friend."

"How do I look?" Leda asked, zipping up her makeup case and replacing it in her purse. "This is the quickest postperformance repair job I've ever done. You don't see any pancake around my hairline, or anything, do you?" She peered into the mirror critically.

"You look fine," Anna reassured her. "Aside from the fact that you're still wearing Madge's pink net bow in you hair."

Leda pursed her lips and ripped the offending ornament from the back of her head. She hadn't been able to see it. "Please tell me if there's anything else," she said to Anna, tossing the bow onto her mirrored tray.

"That's all," Anna said decisively. "You're a knockout. Strong men will faint when you cross their path."

"Just as long as I don't look like I'm coming apart at the seams," Leda answered, grabbing up her coat.

"Even though you feel that way," Anna said, grinning.

"I'll see you later," Leda called over her shoulder, fleeing for the hall.

"Aren't you going to introduce me?" Anna demanded, outraged, her hands on her hips.

"Some other time," Leda replied, and bulleted out the door. If there is another time, she added silently as Reardon turned his head to meet her eyes. He straightened when she came toward him, and his whole demeanor changed as his attention focused on her. Leda felt the pull toward him like a physical thing, the motion of a tide controlled not by the moon but by the force of their mutual attraction. Steady, she thought, taking a deep breath. You've handled three unsuccessful commercial auditions in a row, and you can handle this. She smiled at him and touched his arm. "I'm ready," she said.

"That's quite a change," he observed softly. "Like you stepped into a time warp."

"Did you like the fifties look?" Leda asked, trying to make small talk.

"I liked you in it," he replied, and Leda let the subject drop. He was not a small talker.

"We can go out by the back entrance," she said. "Come this way."

Reardon followed her numbly down the dim staircase, lit only by the red exit sign above the stage door. The lighting was bright enough, however, to reveal Chip Caswell standing at the foot of the stairs, smoking a cigarette.

Leda heaved an inward sigh. What on earth was he doing there? She had turned down his invitation to go out after the show earlier that evening, and now here he was, just in time to catch her sneaking out the rear door with somebody else. An evil genie was overseeing her fate, there was no doubt about it.

"Hi, Chip," she said brightly, speaking first to forestall any inquiries. "Good show tonight. I'll see you tomorrow at rehearsal."

Chip stepped in front of the door, blocking it. Leda could feel Reardon tense as he stood just behind her, almost close enough to touch her.

"I thought you said you were going straight home after the curtain," he greeted her frostily, eyeing Reardon.

"My plans changed, " Leda said evenly, praying that Chip wouldn't choose this occasion for another demonstration of his legendary immaturity. "A friend came to see the show and we decided to go out for a drink." It was easier to give him an explanation he didn't deserve than to deal with the consequences of his wounded ego.

To Leda's astonishment Reardon moved around her and stuck out his hand. "I enjoyed your performance," he said to Chip. "I'm an old friend of Leda's father's, and I thought I'd catch her act. Didn't I see you on television recently?"

Chip preened, hostilities at an end. "Maybe you did," he said fatuously. "I've done some guest shots on series."

Reardon snapped his fingers. "That's it," he said, nodding. "I knew I recognized you."

Leda almost laughed at Chip's expression. He was so lost in his own vanity that he never knew Reardon was manipulating him.

"We'd better go," she interjected. "It's getting late."

"Nice meeting you," Reardon called back, ushering Leda out the door. "I'll look for your name in the credits." They hustled out into the wintry night.

"That was well done," Leda said to Reardon once they were out of Chip's earshot. "Thanks for stepping in like that. I think he was about to become nasty."

"I owed you one," Reardon said, looking down at her.

"Then we're even."

Snow frosted everything, still recent enough to be clean and white. Their footsteps crunched the icy crust as they walked along.

"That guy acts like he has a claim on you," Reardon observed.

"Only in his imagination," Leda answered.

She thought she detected the trace of a smile in Reardon's expression, but it may have been a trick of the streetlight as they passed under it. "He's good looking. I would think women would find him attractive," he said.

"Not this woman," Leda said crisply.

"Why not?" Reardon paused and studied her, waiting for her answer.

Leda tried to think of something innocuous to say. "He wears too much cologne and gold jewelry," she answered, and then cringed. That sounded ridiculous even to her own ears.

But Reardon didn't seem to think so. He nodded and walked on as Leda trotted to catch up with him.

"I don't wear cologne," he said, almost as an afterthought.

"I know."

He cast her a sidelong glance. "And I have no gold jewelry."

"Good."

They looked at each other, not quite smiling. "Where are we going?" he asked, taking in the row of restaurants and shops.

Leda pointed at the Logan Inn across the street. "Right there."

A Christmas tree glowed in the window of the hotel, and a large balsam wreath on the door of the bar enveloped them in its fresh green scent. When Reardon put his arm above Leda's head to push the door open, she stopped walking, lost in the memory of his closeness once before. He barged into her, and then grasped her arms to steady her.

"You okay?" he asked, turning her to look into her face.

"Fine," she responded briskly, tearing her gaze from his and marching ahead of him into the room.

A huge fire blazed in the main bar, with the tree they had seen through the window sending its branches soaring to the ceiling, dripping with tinsel. Reardon took Leda's coat and handed it to the check girl, along with his jacket. They found a spot and sat across from each other at a small round table.

"Nice place," Reardon observed shortly.

"Yes. At this time of year it does a big tourist business, but it's always busy."

His light eyes roamed the room. "I used to think about a place like this at Christmas, roaring fire, big tree—" his gaze touched her face "—pretty girl." Then he shrugged, as if to dismiss the recollection. "What would you like to drink?"

"White wine would be fine," Leda replied softly, trying not to show her reaction to his statement. How lonely he must have been. How lonely he still was; though out of prison, he carried it with him in his mind.

"White wine for the lady, and scotch for me," he said to the waiter who had appeared at his elbow. The man nodded and vanished.

"Would you like to go into the dining room for something to eat?" he asked Leda.

"No, thanks." She smiled. She was usually ravenously hungry after a show, but her appetite had deserted her, along with her customary composure. She felt like a teenager on her first date.

Silence reigned. Finally, Reardon cleared his throat.

"I shouldn't have come here with you," he said huskily, raising his eyes from the table to her face. "It was a mistake. I don't know what to say."

"Why?" Leda asked gently, touched by his candor.

"It's not easy coming out of prison and into social life all at once. I haven't sat down for a drink with a beautiful woman in a long time." He smiled sardonically. "I guess that must be obvious."

That isn't it, Leda thought. It's me. He's uncomfortable with me.

"What's wrong?" she prodded quietly. "You seemed all right when you were outside."

"You weren't facing me then," he answered flatly. "You have your father's eyes. They accuse me."

Leda looked away. "I'm sorry."

"You know what everyone says about me," he persisted. "You know what they say I did."

She met his eyes again. "Yes."

"I thought your aunt would have lost no time in reminding you of the whole story," he said bitterly.

"Did you do it?"

His gaze flickered, as if he'd been hoping she wasn't in any doubt. "That's what they say."

"I'm asking you. What do *you* say?"

The waiter brought their drinks, and Reardon watched him leave before he answered. "Why do you ask me that? Don't you know that every con in prison says he's innocent?" His expression was closed. He didn't expect her to believe him.

"Please talk to me," Leda said, touching his hand where it lay curled on the linen tablecloth. "I want to hear your side of it."

He eyed her warily, unable to credit her interest. "That's more than you could say for everybody else in your town."

"I'm not everybody else. We haven't known each other long, but I think you can tell that already. Can't you?"

His fingers enclosed hers, and that was his answer. Leda waited for him to speak.

"I never would have done anything to hurt your father," he finally said huskily. "I respected him more than anyone else I ever met. He took a chance on me when I was right out of school, without experience, and let me have my head in the lab. He backed up my experiments and never put roadblocks in my way."

"Until he wouldn't let you run that fuel test," Leda said, and then wished she hadn't. He released her hand and sat back stiffly.

"So," he said. "You know all the details."

"I know that you were denied permission, and then ran it anyway. That's when the people were killed."

"That isn't the way it happened!" Reardon burst out, slamming his fist on the table. Several people turned around to look at him, and he subsided visibly, taking a sip of his drink and lowering his eyes.

"How did it happen?" Leda asked calmly.

"That fuel was ready to be tested. The flight was sabotaged." He took in her reaction, his expression stony.

"Sabotaged!" This was the first she'd heard of such a charge.

"I could never prove it, and it didn't come out at the trial. My lawyer said he couldn't raise such a claim if he couldn't support it with evidence, and I had none. But there was someone working for your father who wanted that test to fail, and I think he made sure it did."

"Who?"

"Mike Prescott, one of the other flight engineers. He was jealous; he was always jealous from the day your dad hired me. I was younger, newer, with fresh ideas that your father liked. He knew that I was on to something that might fly, and he killed it, for two reasons. He wanted to finish me, which he did, with a vengeance. And he wanted the formula for himself." Reardon took another deep swallow of the amber liquor in his glass. "I think he took it to another company when your father's business folded."

"How do you know that?" Leda whispered.

Reardon shrugged, swirling the scotch in his tumbler. "Makes sense. He's out in California now, producing some revolutionary new high-octane fuel. Sound familiar? And guess who's out there too. My defense attorney, working for the same outfit."

Leda stared at his sardonic half smile as the enormity of it sunk in.

"You think they were in on it together?" she asked. "That your lawyer railroaded you in order to skip town with his buddy and your stolen formula?"

"Sounds like melodramatic fiction, doesn't it?" Reardon asked, seeing her incredulous expression. He looked away. "I knew you wouldn't believe me."

"I didn't say I didn't believe you. It's just that it's so..."

"Farfetched?" he suggested, downing the last of his drink. "Ridiculous? The sort of fairy tale a convicted felon would weave to defend the indefensible?" His tone was mild, but the knuckles on the hand that held the glass were white with tension.

"It sounds like something that could be true, but only the person it happened to would believe it."

He looked back at her, renewed hope in his eyes. "It is true. I swear it." His voice was deep and steady, filled with utter conviction.

Leda sipped her wine for the first time, wetting her dry lips. He watched her. He didn't seem to be breathing.

"How could your colleague have gotten away with your plans, the results of your research?"

He exhaled slowly, and Leda realized that he had been waiting to see whether her next words would indicate interest or dismissal. He leaned forward and looked into her eyes.

"Easy. With me in jail and your father dead, who would stop him from packing up the lab and walking away with it? He couldn't have counted on what happened to your father, but I'm sure he took full advantage of it." He searched her face. "Prescott had planned to discredit me and then move on, probably waiting awhile to use my plans until the whole affair had died down and your father had retired. Your dad was close to doing that anyway. But when he died, it was a windfall for Prescott, and he used it. No one but your father knew enough about what we were doing to catch on to the piracy." Reardon dropped his eyes and sat back. "I'm sorry about your father. The whole thing was like a nightmare, and when your father died, I guess I sort of gave up." He looked over her shoulder, staring at a point in space. "I don't remember much of what happened after that too well. But I've had years to think while I was locked up, and the only thing that kept me going was planning to come back here and clear my name." His eyes shifted back to hers. "I want the rights to my formula back, and I'm going to get them."

"It must have been difficult for you to return to Yardley," Leda said.

He played with the cocktail napkin on the table. "That's where it happened. The answers must be there too."

Leda studied his spare, grim features. "How can you stand the way people treat you?" she said quietly.

He lifted one shoulder slightly. "I learned in prison that you can get used to almost anything. What I have to do is more important." His lips curled slightly. "I used to be sort of a hothead, rash, impulsive, you know the type. I had to get over that real fast in jail, if I wanted to survive. Now I just let the world go by, as much as I can, unless I'm backed into a corner."

"Were you backed into a corner that night at the Phelps hangar?" Leda asked.

He regarded her levelly. "I thought I was." He turned his head and pressed his lips together. "I couldn't stand the way they were humiliating me in front of you. I can take a lot when I'm alone, but for you to see it..." His voice trailed off into silence.

"I didn't think any less of you," Leda responded, swallowing hard. "I thought less of them. I could see that you were trying very hard to control your temper, but they wouldn't let up on you."

"You'd be surprised how many people think an ex-con is fair game. Especially in your town, when the con is me. I'm not exactly Yardley's most popular resident."

"It must be like walking around with the mark of Cain on your forehead. People won't give you a chance."

"People like your aunt?" Reardon inquired, raising his brows.

"You recognized her at the grave," Leda said.

"She's a hard lady to forget. She was my most outspoken critic during the trial, and I don't imagine she's changed her opinion much."

"She hasn't." Leda narrowed her eyes. "What were you doing at my father's grave that day?"

He shook his head. "I don't know. I guess I wanted to do something, but I didn't know what to do. The flowers were stupid, they were probably dead ten minutes after I left them."

"I don't think that bringing the flowers was stupid," Leda replied. "But you startled me. We didn't see any car, and we thought no one was there."

"I didn't have a car. I walked."

"You walked all the way from town to the cemetery? That's a long trip."

"I don't mind walking, and I like the cold air. It clears my head."

The waiter came back, but Leda declined another round. Her glass was still half full. Reardon waved him away.

"You walk everywhere?" Leda asked.

"Not anymore. I just bought a car." He smiled, a real smile for the first time. It lit his face and crinkled the corners of his eyes. "If you can call what I bought a car. It makes the Edsel look like a triumph of automotive engineering."

Leda laughed, and so did he, a full-throated chuckle, low key but infectious. As Leda sobered she was surprised to feel the sting of tears behind her eyes.

"I think it's a long time since you laughed like that, Mr. Reardon," she said with slight catch in her voice.

"Kyle," he said. "You called me Kyle back at the theater, when you wanted to stop me."

"Kyle," she repeated, smiling at him. He smiled back.

"You're right," he said. "It's a long time since I had a drink with a lady, or laughed. You're helping me back into the world, Leda."

"Thank you. I hope so."

"Your father once told me how he picked your name. He always used to talk about you, when you were away at school. I think he wanted you home."

"Monica insisted on boarding school. She wanted me to be refined."

"You are. But your father wasn't convinced that he'd done the right thing. There's some poem about swans, he said you were named after the girl in it. He used to recite it, and show all of us your pictures."

Leda winced. "Not those pictures I sent from school. They were awful."

"No, they weren't. I liked to see them." He grinned. "I remember one with you in pajamas. You had your arm around another girl, a redhead."

Leda groaned. "I can't believe he was showing that to people. That was taken at a slumber party. We both hadn't slept all night, and we looked it."

"I thought it was cute." His expression became serious. "I knew who you were right away when I saw you in the cemetery. I think I would have known you even if I hadn't seen the photos. You resemble your father."

Leda nodded slowly. "Yes. That's what everybody says."

The grandfather clock in the entry hall of the inn chimed eleven. Reardon looked surprised, as if he had lost track of the time.

"I'd better take you back to your car," he said abruptly. "I have the midnight to eight shift at the hangar."

Leda looked puzzled. "Then why were you working when I was there last week?"

"Oh, I'm switching shifts, filling in whenever they need me." He stood and walked around to her chair, pulling it out.

"That's a difficult schedule to keep," Leda commented, going with him to the hall.

"I was lucky to get the job at all, I can't be choosy about the hours." He paid the bar tab and walked back to the table to leave a tip. Leda stood by while he got their coats and helped her into hers. She thought his hands rested on her shoulders a moment longer than was necessary, but she wasn't sure.

"Where are you parked?" he asked, hunching his shoulders against the cold, which clutched at them the second they stepped out the door. Leda shivered, and he put his arm around her as he guided her across the street.

"In the lot behind the theater. What about you?"

"I came late, had to park in the street, about a half mile down the road," he answered.

"Then go. I don't want you to be late. I can get back to my car by myself."

He looked at her. "Would you rather I left?" he said. He had become tense again, withdrawn.

"Why do you say that?" she asked, confused by his response to her innocent statement.

He paused. "Are you afraid of me?" he said, putting his hands in his pockets and regarding her soberly.

"No, of course not. I just went to the inn with you, didn't I?"

"That's not the same thing as a dark, empty parking lot. There were a lot of people there, and you would feel safe."

"I feel safe right now," she replied softly. "I feel safe with you."

"You're sure?" he insisted.

"I'm sure. Now let's go, or you will be late for work."

They hurried through the freezing air to the almost-deserted lot, and Reardon waited while Leda unlocked the door of her car. She got in and started it, then left it running to warm up, while she got out and stood next to him in the feeble light from the arc lamps overhead.

"Thank you for the drink," she said. "I enjoyed it."

"Did you?" he asked, as if he needed reassurance.

"Of course. And I'm glad you came to see my show." She laughed suddenly. "I'm especially glad you came tonight. A few days ago we had a real disaster, and you're lucky you missed it."

"I like to see you laugh," he said softly, touching her cheek. "It reminds me of what my life used to be like, before everything went wrong."

Leda froze, all her awareness concentrated on the sensation of his warm fingers on her skin. He withdrew his hand quickly, as if he had exceeded some boundary he'd set for himself.

"I really appreciate the way you listened to me," he added.

She started to speak, and he held up his hand.

"It doesn't matter whether you believe every word of it or not," he said. "Just to have somebody listen, and not dismiss me or shout me down, meant a lot."

Leda didn't know what to say.

"Good night," he said quietly.

Leda wanted to ask when she would see him again but held her tongue. "Good night, Kyle," she replied instead, and got into her car. He shut the door, and thumped it once with his palm, as if to send her on her way. She watched him walk back toward the street, resisting the impulse to call after him and tell him that she would give him a ride to his car. He liked to walk in the cold, she reminded herself. It cleared his head. She wished she knew something that would clear hers. It seemed to be filled with thoughts of the man who had just left her.

The next evening Leda received two dozen white roses at the dressing room of the theater. Anna took the box at the door and hovered nearby, crowing when Leda unwrapped the green tissue paper to reveal a profusion of dewy, long-stemmed blossoms inside.

"Who is it from?" she demanded, almost ripping the card out of Leda's hand. The heady perfume from the flowers filled the room.

Leda didn't answer, her expression absorbed. She stroked a rose with a thoughtful forefinger.

"Thank you for last night," Anna read aloud. "I never expected understanding from you of all people, but it's obvious that you share your father's kind nature. Gratefully, Kyle Reardon."

"Flowers like these cost the earth," Leda said softly. "He doesn't have that kind of money. He hardly has any money at all."

"Good taste is what he has," Anna said admiringly, returning the card to the box. "Look at those beauties." She bent over the flowers, inhaling, and then tapped Leda on the shoulder. "'Thank you for last night'?" she quoted, raising her brows.

"We had a drink, Anna, that's all. Sorry to disappoint you."

"Two dozen roses for a drink? You must have made quite an impression."

"I hope so," Leda said, almost to herself. In a louder tone she said, "Do you always regard gifts from men as payment for services rendered?"

It was a line from a terrible play they'd both been in, and Anna laughed. "Kyle Reardon is that guy you left with after the show, right? The tall dark one with the crummy jacket?"

"The jacket isn't crummy. It's just...old."

"Yeah, well, its owner isn't. I'd say he's just about the right age, wouldn't you?"

"Anna, don't you have some lines to go over with Peter? You'd better catch him while he's still vertical."

"All right, all right, don't ever say I can't take a hint." She picked up her script book and swept from the room.

Leda found a vase in the prop closet and filled it with water, arranging the roses into a spray from her vanity table.

He'll call me, she thought. He'll call me soon.

He didn't call. Leda waited for almost three weeks and heard nothing. She looked for him in vain everywhere, but as Christmas approached she realized that he had no intention of getting in touch with her again.

Five

——

"Look out!" Clair yelled as the tree they were carrying swung around and barely missed Leda's head. She ducked, and they propped the Douglas fir against the wall.

"I swear this thing grew in the trunk on the way home," Claire muttered, wiping her brow.

"Come on, Claire, stop grumbling and help me move it inside," Leda urged, getting a better grip on the trunk.

"You insisted on buying the hugest tree in the place," Claire protested.

"I like a big tree."

"Do you like to *carry* a big tree?" Claire demanded rhetorically, panting as they maneuvered the greenery into the designated corner. They let it rest there and retired, gasping, to the adjoining windows.

"Look at that monster," Claire moaned when she had caught her breath. "It belongs in Rockefeller Center."

"Just think how much fun it will be to decorate," Leda said, standing back and admiring the view.

"Kind of like decorating the Yosemite National Forest," Claire replied, but she was smiling too.

They were on the enclosed porch that ran along the back of the duplex. The two women had decided to pool their resources and purchase one Christmas tree, to be dressed and outfitted from their mutual stock of lights and ornaments.

"I'll get the stepladder so we can tie it to the sash, and you get the boxes of stuff from your cellar," Leda said, and Claire nodded. When they reconvened a few minutes later, Claire was dragging two overstuffed cardboard boxes brimming with gaudy baubles.

"Just leave that by the door until we get this bush strung up," Leda said. They concentrated on fixing the tree in place, and when that was done, Leda perched on top of the ladder to start stringing the lights from the top.

"You'll be able to see this from the street in the back," Claire said with satisfaction. "But I still don't know why I let you talk me into this traditional Tannenbaum: my art deco idea would have been much better."

"I'm not into silver-and-black Christmas trees, Claire," Leda replied dryly.

"You're a stick-in-the-mud," Claire sniffed. She handed Leda an extension cord. "So you're going to Monica's for Christmas dinner?" she asked.

"Yes."

"I have to leave for Wilmington tomorrow morning, so we'd better finish this today."

Claire was going home to her parents' house in Delaware for the holiday. "Have you decided about the cast party tomorrow night?" Claire went on, watching Leda's expression.

Leda made a face. "I don't think I'm going to go. Anna invited me, but I just don't feel like seeing all of them. I know that sounds terrible, but Chip will be there and..."

"You'd rather avoid him, especially when he's high on holiday cheer."

"Right. Monica wants me to go to my cousin's house in Wynnewood, but I'll be with the family at her house the next afternoon, and it seems kind of pointless to drive over there for just a few hours."

"So you're planning to spend Christmas Eve sitting here by yourself, wondering why Kyle Reardon hasn't called you."

"Don't start up about that again," Leda answered, plugging one strand of lights into another and testing it.

"I can't help it. When are you going to realize that the man isn't interested in you, and give up?"

"You're wonderful for my ego," Leda mumbled, wrapping a group of bulbs around a branch and clipping the cord into place.

"I'm sorry if that sounded harsh, but you'd better face facts. I agree that it looked very promising at the beginning, but three weeks of silence is hard to overlook. Tomorrow is Christmas Eve. What is he waiting for? New Year's? Easter?"

"I don't know," Leda said irritably. "I guess he's busy, trying to put together his case."

"If he *has* a case," Claire said darkly, pulling apart a knot in the last strand of lights.

"I believe him," Leda said stubbornly. Ever since she'd told Claire about her conversation with Reardon at the inn, the two women had this discussion every time they met.

"Oh, Leda, you'd believe in the tooth fairy if you found a quarter under your pillow. I can see where this guy could be very charming, but the weight of the evidence is stacked heavily against him. And even if he is working night and day to prove his innocence, he could take time out for a two-minute phone call."

Leda didn't answer, crestfallen, and Claire relented. "Look," she said, "I'm only trying to get you to perk up and look elsewhere. You're beautiful and intelligent, you don't have to wait around for this ex-convict to remember you're alive."

"Don't call him that," Leda said in a small voice. "It isn't his fault he went to prison if he was sent there by mistake."

"All right," Claire said, bending to plug the master cord into the socket under the tree. "But look at it this way. It's probably a good thing that you haven't heard from him. With the past against you, it would have been rough going, and he's being smart. So should you." She straightened and went to the wall next to the door, flicking the light switch. The tree burst into life with myriad multicolored stars.

"Beautiful!" she said, clapping her hands.

Leda climbed down to the floor. She went to the box of ornaments and opened one in silence.

Claire bit her lip. "Have you thought about calling him?" she asked her friend.

"I've thought about it," Leda replied. "I haven't done it. Like most people, I have no desire to look foolish. I've already kissed him in public and chased after him through a milling crowd at the theater. I think the next move is his."

"And if he doesn't make it?"

Leda hung a red glass bell on the tree. "Nothing happens, I guess."

"Nothing is happening right now."

"Oh, I disagree," Leda said sarcastically. "I'm driving myself crazy. You can't call that nothing."

Claire sighed. "What do you think about the audition tomorrow morning?" she asked brightly, **trying** to lighten the mood.

Leda had a tryout for an aspirin commercial scheduled for 9:00 A.M.

"I don't know. The way I feel right now, looking pained shouldn't be too difficult, so maybe I'll get it."

Claire handed her a striped candy cane, and Leda hung it on a branch.

"Cheer up," Claire said. "You'll feel better on the holiday, when you see all your family and everyone is together."

Leda nodded, thinking that it would take more than a turkey dinner to raise her spirits this time.

Reardon threw down his screwdriver in frustration and wiped his forehead with the back of his hand. This repair job was not going well, and the cylinder was needed for a flight going out at six o'clock. He took a break and squinted down at his grease-stained fingers, pulling a handkerchief out of his pocket to wipe them off. A theater ticket stub, torn in half, fluttered to the floor as he did. He bent to pick it up, remembering the evening he had spent with Leda Bradshaw.

He should not have gone to see her perform in the play. He especially shouldn't have requested a seat in the front row, where she could spot him when the house lights came up. But he knew why he had done it. He wanted to be up close to her, where he could see every gesture she made, hear every nuance in her voice. And when she asked him to wait for her, he couldn't refuse, though every sensible bone in his body screamed at him to get away from her. And now it was too late. Just as he feared, the few hours in her company had completed the circle of his obsession, and he could hardly think about anything else but their time together at the inn. He went over every word she'd said in his mind, and could recall her facial expressions as if she were sitting right beside him.

With monumental self-discipline he had managed not to contact her, but he was perpetually exhausted, as if the effort of refraining from doing what he most wanted to do was wearing him out. He got through each day—going to work and coming home, eating and trying to sleep, writing letters and making phone calls to get a hearing on his license—feeling only half alive. Life was where Leda was, and he wasn't with her. But for once in his screwed-up, miserable existence, he was going to be unselfish and think of someone else first. She was better off without him, and he was determined to leave her alone.

Reardon looked up as Jim Kendall approached, carrying a yellow pay envelope.

"Here's your overtime check," the plant manager said. "I thought you would want it before the holiday."

"Thanks a lot," Reardon said, accepting the envelope and smiling at Kendall. Reardon liked him. He had taken a chance on hiring a man with a prison record, and unlike some of the other employees, he always treated him fairly.

"How's it coming?" Kendall asked, gesturing to the dismantled cylinder.

"Oh, I'll get it," Reardon replied, shrugging. "It may take awhile, but I'll put it together."

"You usually do," Kendall said, nodding. He studied the younger man while Reardon picked up the screwdriver again and went back to his labors.

"Have you seen anything of the Bradshaw girl lately?" Kendall asked mildly, his tone belying his keen interest.

He saw Reardon stiffen, but he didn't look up. He shook his head silently.

"Too bad," Kendall went on. "That was a nice thing she did for you, breaking up the sideshow like that. You were heading straight for a brawl."

"You saw that?" Reardon asked, raising his head, his gray eyes intent.

"Yeah, I was in back and got wind of what was going on. And even if I hadn't, I would have heard about it. It was all the talk around here, but I'm sure you know that."

Reardon didn't answer, looking back at the work he was doing.

"She's a nice girl, Kyle," Kendall said gently.

Reardon's mouth tightened. "I know she's a nice girl. That's why I'm doing her the biggest favor of her life and staying away from her." He turned away slightly, and it was a dismissal. He didn't want to talk about it.

Kendall strolled back to his office, rubbing the back of his neck thoughtfully.

Reardon was a strange one. With his background, Kendall had expected him to be a problem, surly, possibly belligerent. But he was quiet to the point of reticence, and went out of his way to avoid trouble, doing his job and keeping to himself. And he was exhibiting an uncommon sensitivity in avoiding Leda Bradshaw. He obviously thought he would be bad news for the daughter of his former employer, and Kendall could hardly disagree with him. But Kendall thought it would take more fortitude than he himself possessed to resist the invitation implicit in the girl's gesture that evening at the hangar. She had wanted Reardon, and everyone who witnessed them together knew it.

Kendall sighed. It was a tough situation. Those two were obviously drawn to each other, but Reardon didn't feel he should do anything about it. Poor guy. Kendall had seen enough of him to tell that he was very lonely, the type who'd been alone so long he barely knew what it was to interact with other people beyond the level of necessary conversation. And he'd been shaken by the encounter with Bradshaw's daughter; he'd walked around for the rest of the night in a daze. Yet he chose to pursue his solitary path, working so much overtime that he wasn't away from the job long enough to sleep, much less establish a relationship with Leda Bradshaw or anyone else.

Kendall shook his head. It was none of his business if the man wanted to work himself to death. He doubtless needed the money, and the long hours probably kept his mind off the things he wanted to forget.

Kendall opened the door to his office and hurried to answer his ringing phone, his thoughts shifting back to the business at hand. Out on the floor of the hangar, Reardon worked on the defective cylinder, while the other employees walked a wide circle around him, leaving him, as always, by himself.

When Leda got up in the dark the next morning to get ready for her audition, it was snowing. She turned on the radio to get the local weather, and the news was not good. The snow was expected to continue for several hours, with accumulation of three to four inches and hazardous driving conditions.

She briefly debated whether or not to go out at all, but the debilitated condition of her checking account convinced her to make the trip into New York. The trains would be running, and she had spent too much on Christmas gifts, as usual. When the bills came in next month, she would be having her customary January nervous breakdown, and the thought impelled her into her waterproof boots and out the door.

Claire, the rat, was still sleeping. Her teacher's vacation had already begun, and she would be nice and rested for her trip to Wilmington later in the day. Leda propped her gift, an illustrated volume on impressionist painters, inside her storm door where it would be protected from the weather. Then she trudged down to the street and set about the task of clearing off her car for the drive to the station.

Fifteen minutes later she was on her way, and convinced that she should have stayed home. The roads were treacherous, as smooth as glass, and groaned aloud when she approached the slope down to the Yardley depot and saw that it was blocked by a stalled truck. Other drivers were turning around and crawling back up the hill. Leda reversed direction and headed for the river road, which was bound to be less trafficked and consequently more covered with snow. But there was no alternative; if she wanted to keep her appointment, she had to try.

Leda had almost made it to the train station, creeping along and peering through the curtain of falling snow, when she hit a patch of ice and lost control of the car. The wheel spun out of her hands and the car shot across the road, careering madly into the bushes on the other side. She was alone on the road, or she would surely have been hit. The car plunged down the slope toward the river, and came to rest against the trunk of a large oak at the water's edge. It bumped to a stop, the rear wheels still turning, and Leda slumped in relief, her heart pounding.

It was several minutes before she could bring herself to open her eyes and shut off the engine. She knew there was no hope of jockeying the car out of the ditch; the rear fender pointed into the air at a 45-degree angle, and the whole slope was as slick as buttered corn. She glanced at her watch and sighed. There was no way to make her audition. It would take her hours to get out of this mess, and it would cost plenty to get towed back onto the road. Great idea you had about making some extra money, Leda, she congratulated herself. She gingerly pushed at her door and discovered that it was stuck.

Leda sat and considered her situation. She could either stay there, trapped like an astronaut in a capsule, or she could try to dig her way out and get help. She chose the latter course of action, and reached for the handle of her door.

It was some time before she managed to get it open, and then push it forward enough for her to slither through it. She rested for a while, leaning against the side of the car, and then reached back into the driver's seat for her scarf and mittens. She slipped her purse strap over her left arm and squared her shoulders for the walk.

As the hour got later traffic would pick up, and she had hopes of hitching a ride. But first she had to get to the road. Climbing out of the gully proved to be a tricky proposition, and she was glad her boots had gripping soles. Once out on the street, she began flagging down passing cars, which were still few and didn't stop. Finally a farmer from Upper Makefield gave her a ride in his pickup, taking her the two miles to the closest gas station. The tow trucks available there were already out, however, and promised to be gone all morning. Leda was thinking that the story would probably be the same at every station in town when an idea struck her. Her father had always kept towing equipment out at the hangar, for company problems, not for commercial rental. Maybe the truck was still there, and maybe Phelps would send it out for her.

She asked to use the pay phone at the station and called her agent, explaining why she wouldn't be showing up for her audition. Then she called the office at the hangar and got Jim Kendall. She was in luck. He said he would send a man out for her as soon as possible. Leda got a cup of coffee from a vending machine and sat in a folding chair to wait, thinking that the appeal of winter's beauty had been somewhat dimmed by this experience.

Leda was watching through the window of the gas station when the Phelps truck pulled into the lot and came to a halt. The man who got out was suspiciously tall and slim, and she caught a glimpse of a stern, handsome profile and snow-frosted dark hair as he walked to the glass enclosure where she sat. It was Reardon.

"Are you all right?" he greeted her. "You weren't hurt?"

"I'm fine," she replied. "I wish I could say the same for my car."

"Tell me what happened," he said, narrowing his eyes against the driving snow. Leda stepped aside to let him walk past her into the small heated room and he unzipped his jacket, eyeing her coffee with longing. Leda handed it to him wordlessly, and he drank it while she told him the story of her morning's adventure.

"So it's wedged into a ditch, out by the river, is that right?" he said when she finished.

"That's about the size of it. Sorry."

"No problem. Let's get to it. Can you show me where it is?"

"I think so."

He gestured toward the truck. "We'll see if we can get it out for you."

As they walked across the lot Leda glanced at him and said, "I didn't know Jim would send you."

"Why not? I work for him," Reardon answered shortly. He didn't look at her.

Leda was trying hard not to show her disappointment at his cold reception, but it was proving a difficult task. She'd thought they had established a rapport at their last meeting, but he was acting as though she were any stranger who needed his professional services. She didn't know the reason for his change in attitude, but she did know she didn't like it.

He helped her into the cab of the truck, and followed her directions to the abandoned car. He parked the truck and got out with her, studying the position of the car.

"I should have brought another man," he said finally, turning to her and shaking his head. "I didn't know how bad this was. I'm not sure I can handle it alone."

"I didn't give Jim the details. I guess I should have, I'm sorry."

"Stop apologizing," he said curtly. "I'll give it a try, I'm just not promising any results."

"I wasn't expecting any promises," she replied tartly, in the same vein. "I know the car's in a tough spot."

He looked at her then, his expression unreadable, and Leda faced him down, holding his eyes with hers. He looked away first.

"Stay here," he said to her, starting down the slope. "I have to back the truck to the edge and attach the tow chain. Just keep out of the way."

"All right, I will!" she almost yelled, perilously close to breaking down. Why was he treating her this way? She wished Kendall had sent someone else. She watched as he moved the truck into position and inched down the slope to fix the chain to the bumper of her car. As he was turning away to come back to the road, the snow crust gave way beneath his feet and he slipped. Leda watched in horror as he slid the few feet back to the car and sprawled full length, striking his head on the bumper.

He dropped to the snow and lay perfectly still. Sliding and falling, Leda scrambled down the incline. Kneeling next to him, she lifted his head to her lap. She gasped, her heart sinking, when she saw that he was bleeding.

"Kyle, are you all right? Kyle, can you hear me? Oh, why did I let you try this by yourself?" She was half sobbing, almost incoherently, terrified.

After a few seconds he stirred and blinked, attempting to sit up. Leda pushed him down again, overwhelmed with relief.

"Stay there," she ordered. "Don't move."

He looked up at her, putting his fingers to the gash on his forehead, his eyes widening when they came away stained with blood.

"That was some shot on the head," he murmured, struggling to get up again. "I must have been out for a couple of seconds." He shrugged off her restraining arms and lurched to his feet, fishing in his breast pocket for a wad of tissues, which he held to the cut. He squinted up the slope, looking toward the road.

"I'd better try it from another angle," he said. "I don't think I can get the car out this way."

"Oh, will you forget about the lousy car!" Leda yelled, and burst into tears. Reardon stared at her, astonished.

"What's wrong with you?" he asked her.

"What's wrong with me! I thought you were really hurt, that's what's wrong with me. Not that you care, you've been treating me like a communicable disease since you saw me. Go on back to your engines and ask Kendall to give some other poor slob this dirty detail." She turned her back on him and cried into her scarf.

Seconds later she felt a touch on her shoulder. "Kendall didn't give me this dirty detail," Reardon said in her ear. "When I heard you might be in trouble, I volunteered."

Leda faced him, looking into his eyes, lost in them. The snow swirled around them, enclosing them in drifting whiteness, like two figures in a crystal paperweight.

"I didn't mean to treat you like a disease," he said softly. "I was just trying to fight the feeling..." He traced the path of a tear on her cheek with a hard forefinger, and then bent to catch the drop of wetness with his tongue. Leda closed her eyes. In the next instant his mouth came down on hers.

His lips were cold, but warm inside when he opened them. Leda responded helplessly, clutching at the lapels of his jacket, returning his kisses with all the pent-up longing of their time apart.

Reardon's hands roamed over her hair, her neck, her face, as his mouth moved to her brow, her cheek, and back to her lips again. Leda wound her arms around his waist, trying to blend her body with his, and the barrier of their heavy clothing frustrated both of them.

"I want to touch you," Reardon rasped, pulling at the belt of her coat. Leda stepped back and let him loosen it, sagging in his arms as he enfolded her again, running his hands under her sweater, seeking her skin.

"My hands are cold," he whispered, hesitating, and she pressed against them, reveling in the feel of his hard palms and strong fingers on her soft flesh.

"I'll warm them," she responded, and he groaned, turning her to cup her breasts, clad only in a scrap of lace. Leda arched against him, resting her head on his shoulder, and he nudged her hair aside to kiss her neck.

"Let's go up into the cab," he murmured, pushing her toward the road and the waiting truck.

"The cab?" she repeated, uncomprehending, stunned by the suddenness and the force of his lovemaking.

Reardon looked up, taking in their location and the weather as if he had forgotten their surroundings. It was painfully clear that there was no place to go. Realization of the insane situation dawned on him, and he let Leda go.

"What am I doing?" he muttered. "Look where we are, I must be crazy. I'm treating you like some..."

"No, you're not," Leda said, grabbing his hands. "You're not alone, Kyle, this is happening to me too."

"It shouldn't be happening to either one of us," he said firmly, and took her arm to hurry her along. "Come on. I'm taking you home, and then I'll come back with one of the other guys and get your car. It'll be dropped off later, once we tow it out."

Leda allowed him to usher her back to the tow truck, the difficulty of the climb making conversation nearly impossible. But once she was installed in the passenger seat, and he was driving across town to her apartment, she tried again.

"Aren't we even going to talk about it?" she asked him, staring straight ahead into the cascading snow.

"No. Talking never does any good. I want you to forget it, and I will too."

"Do you think that will be easy?" she demanded, turning her head to look at him.

He wouldn't meet her glance, but kept looking forward at the road. "Easy or not, it has to be done."

"Why?" she demanded. "Just because you say so?"

"Because of who you are, and who I am, and the situation we're in. It's all wrong, and you know it."

"I only know how I feel," she said miserably, directing him to turn at her corner. "I don't know what's going to happen in the future any more than you do, but I'm willing to take a chance."

He pulled up in front of her house, staying in the middle of the street to avoid the drift that was already gathering at the curb. He put the truck in neutral and turned in his seat, finally facing her.

"You have no idea what you're talking about," he said quietly. "You have no concept of what it's like living my life. I can't share that with anybody, I can hardly bear it myself. Get out while you can, Leda, and don't look back."

She looked into his eyes, pleading, but he turned his head away.

"Do you want me to walk you to your door?" he asked. "It's very slippery, and you might fall."

"I'll be fine," Leda answered, lifting her chin. "Thanks for coming out to get me." She jumped down from the cab and looked up at him, ensconced behind the wheel, one hand on the gear shift, ready to go.

"Merry Christmas," she said, and slammed the door.

She watched as he drove off down the street, at a snail's pace like the rest of the vehicles on the road, and then trudged through the snow to her door, too drained to cry.

The snow stopped falling around noon and the sun came out, its brilliance reflected from every surface with blinding brightness. The plows and sanders appeared, grinding and dragging past Leda's windows, clearing the roads. The radio announcer kept interrupting the Christmas carols with cheery bulletins about how traffic would be flowing freely in time for holiday traveling. Since Leda planned to go nowhere, she finally turned off the radio and switched to tape cassettes, desiring to skip the happy chatter between songs.

She spent the afternoon baking compulsively, making five dozen Christmas cookies to take to Monica's the next day. She wanted to be busy in order to drive Reardon from her mind. But her thoughts still ran while her hands worked. She ended up with a mound of goodies fit for the throne of the Ghost of Christmas Present, but without the inner peace traditionally promised for such a special night.

At five o'clock she gave up and took a shower, sitting in front of the television to brush out her wet hair. She switched it on and was treated to several minutes of *Christmas in Connecticut*, a holiday oldie starring Barbara Stanwyck and a festively decorated New England farm. Leda turned off the set and went into the kitchen to make tea.

As she was filling the kettle with water she caught sight of the piles of pastry stars and wreaths and trees, all frosted and ready to be eaten, all dressed up with no place to go. Leda put down the teapot with a bang.

She was not going to wait for that stupid, stubborn man to realize he needed her. She felt it in his kiss that morning, and he couldn't deny what he had told her in that most basic form of communication, no matter what he said with words.

Leda went into her bedroom and dried her hair, getting dressed and selecting a sheet of wrapping paper from the stack on her desk. She returned to the kitchen and put together a plate of cookies, wrapping it with the gold foil and finishing off the package with a red velvet bow.

Reardon had come to her aid that morning. There was no harm in bringing him a little gift to show her appreciation.

Leda put on her coat and snatched up her keys with a determined smile.

Kyle Reardon was in for a visitor this Christmas Eve.

And it wasn't going to be Santa Claus.

First Class Romance

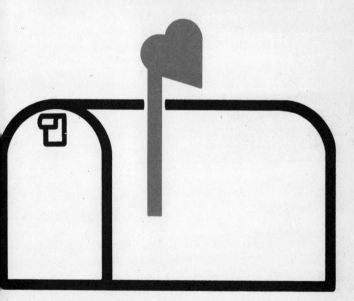

Delivered to your door by

Silhouette Desire®

(See inside for special 4 FREE book offer)

Find romance at your door with 4 FREE Silhouette Desire novels!

Now you can have the intense romances you crave without searching for them. You can receive Silhouette Desire novels each month to read in your own home. Silhouette Desire novels are modern love stories for readers who want to experience firsthand *all* the joyous and thrilling emotions of women who fall in love with a passion that knows no bound. You can share in the passion and joy of their love, every month, when you subscribe to Silhouette Desire.

By filling out and mailing the attached postage-paid order card, you'll receive FREE 4 new Silhouette Desire romances (a $9.00 value) plus a FREE Mystery Gift. You'll also receive an extra bonus: our monthly Silhouette Books Newsletter.

Approximately every 4 weeks, we'll send you 6 more Silhouette Desire novels to examine FREE for 15 days. If you decide to keep them, you'll pay just $11.70 (a $13.50 value) with no charge for home delivery and at no risk! You'll also have the option of cancelling at any time. Just drop us a note. Your first 4 books and the Mystery Gift are yours to keep in any case.

Silhouette Desire ®

A FREE
Mystery Gift
awaits you, too!

FILL OUT THIS POSTPAID CARD AND MAIL TODAY!

Mail this card today for your
4 FREE BOOKS
(a $9.00 value) and
a Mystery Gift FREE!

Silhouette Desire ®

Silhouette Books, 120 Brighton Rd., P.O. Box 5084, Clifton, NJ 07015-9956

☐ Yes, please send 4 new Silhouette Desire novels and a Mystery Gift to my home FREE and without obligation. Unless you hear from me after I receive my 4 FREE books, please send me 6 new Silhouette Desire novels for a free 15-day examination each month as soon as they are published. I understand that you will bill me a total of just $11.70 (a $13.50 value) with no additional charges of any kind. There is no minimum number of books that I must buy, and I can cancel at any time. No matter what I decide, the first 4 books and the Mystery Gift are mine to keep.

NAME _____
(please print)

ADDRESS _____

CITY _____ STATE _____ ZIP _____

Terms and prices subject to change.
Your enrollment is subject to acceptance by Silhouette Books.

CAD525

Six

It was a clear, cold night, serenely still, the stars scattered like chips of ice against a dark expanse of frigid sky. The air was crisp and clean, like chilled Chablis, and the scent of woodsmoke drifted through it from the neighborhood chimneys, adding a subtle note to the bouquet. Leda inhaled deeply, pulling her collar closer around her neck. Thus fortified, she walked down to the street to examine the damage on her car.

There was one big dent with several scratches, which didn't look too bad by the feeble light from the streetlamps but might be a startling revelation on Christmas morning. A Phelps van had arrived in the middle of the afternoon, with her car trailing behind it, driven by a teenager who knocked on her door and handed over the keys she'd left with Reardon. When Leda asked about the towing bill, the kid shook his head and said that Mr. Kendall wanted him to tell her it was "on the house." He loped off and got into the van, which drove away.

There was no sign of Reardon.

Leda unlocked her door and set the package carefully on the floor in the back, guarding against the sudden stops, likely in this weather, that might turn her offering into bird seed by the time she arrived. Then she got in front and steered the little car cautiously onto the icy road, skittish about driving after the incident that morning. She took it slow, and as the distance to Sara Master's house was not far, Leda found herself pulling to stop across from the two-story colonial before she had formulated what whe wanted to say to Reardon. She shut off the engine and stared into space, unable to come up with a witty entry line, or even an entertaining explanation for her presence. She invariably turned into a brainless dolt in emotional moments; after the fact, she could always invent charming and interesting repartee, but at the required time she drew a blank. She was drawing one now, so she surrendered and examined the lower floor of the house, occupied by Sara and her husband. It was brightly lit, and the Christmas tree in the bay window blazed like a torch, so Leda concluded glumly that the Masters were home. She was hoping that they might be out, so that her visit would have a better chance of going unobserved. But there was a light in Reardon's apartment too. Her father had always closed the hangar early on Christmas Eve, and Phelps had apparently maintained the custom.

Leda started the car again and parked it around the corner, away from Sara's prying eyes. She wasn't ashamed of her interest in Reardon, but if Sara saw her, she would definitely tell Monica. A Christmas

Day confrontation with her aunt, in front of an audience of staring relatives, was to be avoided at all costs. Leda locked the doors and walked back to the house, quietly taking the exterior stairway to the second floor. Clutching her package like a good luck charm, she knocked on Reardon's door.

She could hear music coming from the apartment, but there was no answer to her summons. She knocked again, harder, and after a few moments Reardon pulled the door open, barefoot and shirtless, clad only in a pair of corduroy jeans. His lips parted in surprise when he saw Leda.

"Hello, Kyle," she greeted him. "This is for you." She extended the package she held.

He stared at it, then at her. "A Christmas present?" he said.

"A thank-you gift. For your heroic rescue."

He snorted. "It was hardly heroic. It wasn't even a rescue. But thanks anyway, I appreciate it." He took the plate and they looked at each other.

"May I come in?" Leda asked primly, seeing that he was not going to cooperate. She knew he wasn't rude; he would invite her inside if she asked him to do so.

"Oh, I'm sorry," he answered, stepping back to let her pass. "It must be freezing out there."

Leda walked into the small apartment, and he shut the door behind her. She glanced around at the spare furnishings, the Spartan decor and her eye settled on the roaring fire on the hearth, the only element of warmth and cheer in the room.

"The fire is lovely, just the thing on such a cold night," she said.

He nodded, putting his hands in his pockets and watching her. He was obviously uncomfortable, and she was beginning to wish she had stayed at home with Barbara Stanwyck.

"No tree?" she asked brightly, examining the empty corners of the room.

"I got a tree," he said flatly, jerking his thumb at the top of the battered stereo. It was a plastic, lop-sided silver imitation, about a foot high, with lackluster, tarnished decorations. God only knew where he had gotten it, but the sight of it made Leda want to cry. She quickly turned away and looked at him, which was a mistake.

The hard beauty of his body made her mouth go dry with longing. His smooth, muscular arms and shoulders, covered by a matte expanse of satiny skin, begged for her touch. His broad chest, roughened by fine dark hair like that on his head, tapered to a narrow waist, and she could see the sturdy muscles of his abdomen, flat and firm under the closure of his jeans. Her eyes moved slowly to his face, and she could tell that he knew what she was thinking. She gradually became aware that the stereo was playing a song she had heard before, but which took on new meaning in this context. Reardon's gaze moved from her lips, down to her body, enshrouded in her duffel coat, and back to her mouth again as the singer intoned the low, intimate lyrics:

> "I wake up at night
> with the sheets soaking wet,
> and a freight train running
> through the middle of my head,
> Only you can quench my desire,

Oh oh oh, I'm on fire."

Reardon swallowed hard, walked directly to the stereo, and switched it off. A heavy silence filled the room.

"Please excuse the mess," Reardon finally said, clearing his throat. "I wasn't expecting company. How come you aren't at a party or something tonight?"

"Oh, well, I was invited to one, but I thought I'd visit you instead."

His eyes narrowed. "Why? Is this your good deed in honor of the day? Dispense a little charity to the local pariah?"

Leda turned on her heel. "I didn't mean to intrude on your privacy. I'll go."

She hadn't taken two steps before he was at her side, his long fingers closing over her arm. "Leda, please stay. I'm sorry. I seem to suspect everyone's motives these days." He shrugged helplessly, shaking his head. "Being alone so much has turned me into quite a boor. I wasn't always this way, I assure you."

"I believe that," she said softly, meeting his eyes. "But I wish you would see that not everyone is out to get you."

"I'm beginning to see that you're not," he replied with the trace of a smile. He released her arm and gestured to a chair. "Let me have your coat, and take a seat. I'll make some coffee, okay?"

"Okay," Leda agreed as he helped her out of her coat, charmed by his awkward attempt to play host. He tossed her coat on an overstuffed sofa, which, along with two chairs, a desk, and the battered kitchen set next to the stove, comprised all the furniture in the room. She could see a bedroom beyond, equally spare.

With quarters like these, no wonder he spent so much time at work.

"What's that I smell?" she asked, sniffing the air.

"Stew," he replied. "I was just making dinner." He walked over to the stove and stirred something in a pot.

She watched what he was doing, and realized that "making dinner" consisted of heating up a can of prepared stew. "Maybe I can help," she suggested. "Have you got any eggs?"

He turned back to her. "Sure."

"Cheese, butter, tomatoes, onions?" she went on, and he smiled.

"I think so," he said.

"Fine. How about some omelets?"

He gestured to the tiny kitchenette, which consisted of a series of ancient, mismatched appliances strung together along one wall. "Be my guest."

Leda went to work, and while she was removing items from the refrigerator she noticed that he picked up a sweatshirt folded on a shelf and pulled it over his head. Clothing made him look slim and rangy, disguising his strong, muscular build. In the jeans and pullover, he resembled a college kid ready for an afternoon of touch football.

"These will be ready in just a minute," she called over her shoulder, wondering what he was doing. When she turned to look she saw that he was clearing a space on the scarred maple drop leaf table, shifting piles of books and pamphlets from its surface to the sofa.

"What is all that stuff?" she asked as he came to her side and removed a couple of plates from the cupboard above her head, handing them to her.

"I've been reading up on the procedure for getting my license back," he replied. "You know the government, a million forms and a sea of red tape." He led her to the table and they sat together. He jumped up suddenly and returned with silverware and two napkins.

"Sorry," he said, depositing the things on the table. "I'm not exactly equipped to entertain. I eat by myself, and it's more like the Boy Scout Jamboree around here than the epitome of gracious dining."

"What do you eat when you're alone?" she asked, taking a bite.

He shrugged. "Yogurt, cottage cheese, ice cream, anything you can devour straight from the container. He cut into his omelet and swallowed a large piece. His eyes widened.

"Hey, this is real good," he said, digging in with gusto. His was twice as large as Leda's and he made short work of it.

"Thank you. One of the benefits of a boarding school education. You become an expert at making anything that can be prepared on a hotplate," Leda replied dryly.

He grinned, and her heart turned over. What a smile. She could easily fall into the trap of trying to elicit it.

Leda finished, and when she got up to clear the dishes he waved her away.

"This I can do," he said, scraping the dishes and putting them in the sink. "And I can make coffee. I make it every day." He proceeded to do so, filling the pot at the sink and plugging the percolator into the wall. When he was done he dragged both of his chairs in front of the fireplace and gestured for her to sit in one of them.

"The package I brought is cookies," Leda said. "Maybe you'd like some for dessert."

"Great," he said, looking around the room. "I'll get them." He paused. "What did I do with them?"

"I think you put the plate on the table by the door." Leda responded, amused and touched by his efforts to entertain her. He was eager, almost boyish, in his enthusiasm, and it was a side of him she had never seen. He returned with the plate and gave it to her.

"Do you have any family?" she asked as he got out the cups for the coffee.

"None left around here," he answered. "My parents are both dead and I was an only child. I have some aunts and cousins on my mother's side out in Ohio, but I..." He trailed off, and then resumed. "I haven't heard from them since I went to jail."

"Oh," she said, unsure how to respond. "That's too bad."

He shrugged. "I've become the relative nobody wants to recognize. Before all this happened to me, I never really understood what it means to be the black sheep of the family." He joined Leda in front of the fire, pouring out the coffee. "I hope this stuff is all right," he said, gesturing to the steaming drink. "I'm the only one who ever drinks it, and I'm used to it."

"It's fine," Leda answered, taking a sip and returning the mug to the tray. Reardon disdained the chair across from her and sat at her feet on the small hearth rug, opening up the package she'd brought.

"You made these?" he asked, popping a wreath into his mouth.

"Yes."

"They're fantastic," he mumbled, swallowing a frosted star. "You're really a good cook."

"No, I'm not," Leda said, laughing. "Omelets and cookies are the extent of my repertoire. I can't offer a well-rounded menu with only two dishes."

"That's two more than I can make," Reardon said philosophically, drinking his coffee. He bent his head to put the cup on the floor, and the firelight danced in his dark hair, making it glow with highlights. He looked very young, Leda thought once more, the customary care lines wiped from his face as he sampled goodies like a guilty child.

"Are you warm enough?" he asked suddenly. "My heater is broken again, I have to make time to fix it. The fire is good for me, but..."

"The fire is wonderful," Leda answered. She watched as he put another log on it, stirring the the embers below the blaze with a poker. "Do you always fix anything that breaks?" she asked him.

He nodded. "Just about," he said. "It's a good thing too, because I can't afford repairs. I got a lot of experience tinkering around with appliances in prison."

"You did?" Leda asked.

"Yeah, they had to find a job for me, you know, they pay you two cents an hour or something according to state law. So I was the fixit man, and they kept me pretty busy." He smiled sardonically. "A lot of things get broken in the joint."

"How is everything working out for you at Phelps?" Leda asked quietly.

He looked up at her. "All right. Kendall is fair, and the work keeps me busy."

"Do you think you'll get your license back?"

A shadow crossed his face. "I don't know. Right now it doesn't look too good. The powers that be aren't too high on criminals flying the friendly skies."

"But what if you could prove that you were innocent of the charges?" Leda asked.

"It would be a different story, if I could prove that," he answered evenly. "But at the moment I'm just a guy who did time trying to convince the board that I've reformed." He snorted. "From the replies I've been getting, something tells me they're not buying my act."

"What will you do if you can't work in your field?" Leda said softly.

He spread his hands, staring into the fire. "I'm trying not to consider that possibility," he answered quietly. "The only thing that's kept me going is the idea that someday this will all be over and I'll be able to go back to my career."

"I'm sure that's true," Leda whispered.

He looked up at her with a faint smile. "You just keep telling me that, saddle shoes."

She laughed. "What?"

He smiled wider at her reaction. "Saddle shoes. You look like one of those girls at football games, in short skirts and saddle shoes, rooting for the home team."

"Oh, dear. Do I really?" she said, shaking her head.

"You do to me. The untouchable, the unattainable, the sweetheart of Sigma Chi."

"I'm touchable, Kyle," Leda replied quietly. She wasn't sure he heard her. He stood abruptly and refilled his cup, asking her if she wanted more. When she shook her head, he resumed his spot on the rug, examining her with his head tilted to one side.

"So tell me about yourself," he said. "How did you get into acting?"

"Oh, I got the bug in high school, appearing in plays. Then I went to college and signed up for a drama major without telling my aunt. When I finally announced my intention to become an actress, she reacted as if I'd told her I planned to pursue a career as a streetwalker."

Reardon choked on his coffee. Leda watched as he sputtered and then got himself under control, trying desperately not to break up.

"Oh, go ahead and laugh," she said gloomily. "Everybody else thinks it's hilarious too. I'm tempted every day to give it up and get a safe, sensible job, especially when I give a bad performance and everything goes wrong."

"Don't give it up," he answered seriously. "I think you're very talented. All you need is some more experience, and the right breaks. After seeing you in the play, I can't imagine your doing anything else."

Leda bit her lip, too moved to speak. He was the first person outside of her colleagues in the theater who had offered her any encouragement. Monica treated Leda's ambitions as some sort of bizarre phase she was going through, and even her friends regarded her performances with lighthearted indulgence that annoyed her. Only Claire supported her, but Claire had never seen her in a show.

"Leda?" Reardon inquired, concerned at her silence.

"Yes?" she answered, blinking.

"I could tell that you really love to perform," he went on. "Why? What does it feel like when you're up there?"

"It's a feeling of power, I guess." Trying to express in words what she felt was difficult. "Everyone is watching you, listening to you, and it seems that you have them in the palm of your hand. On stage, you can't see the audience, but that hush tells you they're out there. And when you get that response from them, a sigh, a laugh, a round of applause, well, for me it's the greatest rush in the world." She smiled a little, slightly embarrassed at the torrent his question has unleashed. "Do you understand what I mean?"

He nodded. "I think so. I know that feeling of accomplishment, fulfillment." He looked away. "Flying is like that for me."

"Oh, Kyle." Leda put aside the tray on her lap and knelt next to him on the floor. "You'll fly again. I know it."

"Do you, saddle shoes?" he said softly, reaching out to touch her hair. Leda closed her eyes.

In the next instant he was on his feet. "I think you'd better go," he said hoarsely.

Leda rose also, more slowly, stunned at his abrupt dismissal. She searched his face, and he turned his head.

"Don't look at me like that," he said.

"How am I looking at you?"

"As if I'd...slapped you, or something." He shook his head. "Just go, Leda. Don't ask for trouble."

"Is that what I'm doing?"

"Yes, yes," he said, throwing up his hands. "Bringing me a gift, being so nice to me. What do you think that does to me? Do you know what it means to somebody who's been shut up in jail, a man, to have a beautiful woman take such an interest? Maybe you're just trying to be kind, but—"

"I'm not trying to be kind," Leda cut him off, touching his arm and stepping closer to him. "Kyle, why are you telling me to go? I think you want me to stay."

He gripped her shoulders suddenly and looked down at her, examining her face. "Why did you come here tonight?" he demanded huskily. "Why?"

"I think you know why," she whispered, mesmerized by the silvery eyes boring into hers.

"Tell me," he said.

"I'm falling in love with you," she said quietly.

He let her go instantly, turning his back. "Don't say that," he ground out, agonized.

"I have to say it," Leda answered passionately, stepping around him to face him again. She waited until he met her eyes, and then continued. "I'm not like you, I can't hold everything inside and deny my feelings. Why do you think I'm here? You're the first man I've ever visited without an invitation, I don't *do* things like this. I can't even believe I came. But I missed you so, and when I saw you today, and you kissed me—"

"Don't," he barked. It was a command. She stopped. Kyle held up his hand. "The past stands between us. Until I can prove my innocence I have nothing to offer you."

"You can offer yourself. That's all I want."

He shook his head. "You're dreaming, Leda. This isn't some romantic play where the hero and the heroine solve everything neatly by the curtain. This is real life, and in real life I'm a dead end, a loser, a convicted felon with no future and no prospects. Go home, Leda, and forget me."

"I can't forget you, and I won't," she replied, blinking back tears. "I want to feel the way you made me feel this morning. I want you to kiss me again and make me forget everything but the way we are together. Doesn't that count for anything? Is that so easy for you to dismiss?"

He held her gaze, his eyes tortured, and then he looked away. In that fraction of a second before he turned, Leda saw a glimmer of insecurity, a shadow that told her he wasn't being completely honest with her. Perhaps he believed everything he had just said, but there was something else, something more, he wasn't revealing.

"Kyle, what is it?" she whispered.

He didn't answer.

"You can tell me." She reached for his hand.

He pulled away. "Leave me alone."

"Is that what you really want?"

He remained obdurate, not looking at her.

"What is so awful that you can't say it?"

"All right!" he exclaimed furiously. He faced her, his expression mocking. "You know those guys at the hangar who were giving me a bad time, the charter customers who were making fun of me the night you were there?"

"Yes," Leda said, confused. What was he talking about?

"Well, they were right."

"Right?" she replied, still puzzled.

"Yeah," Reardon went on, frustrated at her lack of understanding. "I haven't had a woman in over four years."

Leda's lips parted. She was beginning to catch his drift.

"Got it now?" he asked sarcastically.

"I think so," she whispered.

"It would be like the first time for me all over again," he went on, flushing deeply, unable to look at her.

"You mean if you made love to me?" she said softly.

He swallowed with difficulty. "I refuse to make a fool of myself," he said. "Not with you." He raised his eyes to hers. "Especially not with you."

Leda was speechless, deeply touched. His insecurity was endearing, but totally unnecessary, and she found it almost amusing. She'd seen him turn enough female heads, including her own, to know that it was unfounded, but she could hardly reassure him on such a delicate subject. She remained silent, unable to think of a thing to say.

"Satisfied?" he asked nastily. "I feel ridiculous, so you can run along now. Your mission is accomplished."

"Kyle, I didn't mean to pry..."

"Yeah, well, you did. Give it up and run back to Auntie, little girl, you're not equipped to deal with my problems."

Stung, Leda picked up her coat and made for the door. She didn't know how to handle his sensitivity, and she just seemed to be making everything worse. She had only taken a couple of steps, however, when he caught up to her and spun her around to face him.

"Don't go," he said urgently. "I didn't mean it, don't go." He pulled her into his arms and kissed her wildly, his mouth warm and pliant, devouring hers. Leda melted into him, her coat falling to the floor. But just as she was winding her arms around his neck, he pulled away, his face a study in conflicting emotions.

"What?" she almost wailed. Surely he couldn't be holding her off again.

He didn't respond, his breathing ragged, his chest heaving.

"Answer me!" she cried. "I've been straight with you, don't I have a right to expect the same honesty in return? Do you want me, or not?"

He stared at her as if she had lost her mind. "How could you even think I don't want you?" he asked in a tone that suggested the idea was absurd. "I've wanted you from the first moment I saw you in a cloud of swirling snow, and every second since."

Leda sobbed, and sagged against him He held her gently, and after a short while she looked up at him and touched his face tenderly.

"Oh, darling, that's all I wanted to hear. I don't care what happened in the past or how long it's been since you...made love. In fact, I'm glad you told me, because it will be like a new beginning with us, a chance to start over fresh."

"I'll be awkward," he murmured, burying his face in her hair and running his hands over her body.

"You could never be awkward at anything," she answered as he raised his head and looked into her eyes.

"I want to please you," he said huskily, and she sank her fingers into the curls at the nape of his neck, pulling his mouth down to hers.

"Oh, shut up," Leda muttered, silencing him with a kiss.

This time there was no hesitation. Reardon reacted powerfully, taking the initiative and kissing her until she was weak and hanging onto him, barely standing. He picked her up in one economical motion, gathering her into his arms and carrying her into the bedroom.

Reardon meant to set her down gently, taking his time. But when Leda fell back upon the pillow, her arms above her head, the look she gave him was so evocative, an enticing combination of innocence and seduction, that he was lost. He forgot his good intentions and dropped onto the bed with her, engulfing her slight body with his heavier one, pressing her into the mattress.

Leda wound herself around him, sighing and closing her eyes. He started to say something, and she shushed him.

"Just hold me," she said, smoothing his soft hair. He obeyed, tightening his grip and dropping his head to her shoulder.

"I dreamed of this so many times," she whispered.

Reardon kissed her neck and looked into her eyes. Leda had never seen him so close before; his silvery irises reflected the moonlight streaming through the window like a cat's.

"I love your face," Leda said, tracing his features with the fingers of one hand as if she were blind. "I think you're very handsome."

His lips opened as she touched his mouth, and he set his teeth gently on the edge of her thumb. "I'm not handsome, Leda," he answered, smiling slightly. "But I'm glad you feel that way."

"Oh, you don't know what I mean," she said, withdrawing her hand. "You're not a woman."

"That's true," he said, laughing softly, kissing the tip of her nose. "And I've never been happier about that than I am at this moment."

Leda had to laugh too, but she sobered quickly as his lips moved lower, capturing hers and driving everything but the thought of him from her mind. He kissed her over and over again, with the deep hunger of long denial. When he sat up to remove his sweat-shirt, Leda sat up with him, and embraced him as soon as he had pulled the top over his head. He inhaled sharply as she kissed his chest, running her tongue over his collarbone and the flat hard nipples, sur-rounded by soft dark hair. His fingers curled around the nape of her neck and he raised her head, seeking her mouth with his. Leda kissed him back with reck-less abandon, unable to touch him, caress him, enough. When he reached for the buttons of her blouse, his fingers trembled, and Leda caught his hand and raised it to her lips.

"I'll do it," she said, and he watched, riveted, as she removed her blouse and dropped it on the floor. He pulled her back into his arms immediately, unhook-ing her bra and tossing the scrap of lace aside. Push-ing her down on the bed, he took one rosy nipple in his mouth. His hand enclosed Leda's other breast, and his fingers brushed the sensitive tip, caressing her with increasing ardor until Leda arched her back and groaned.

"Sweet," he murmured. "So sweet." He planted a row of kisses on her abdomen, pushing aside the waistband of her slacks to insert his tongue in her na-val. Leda gasped, tossing her head on the pillow.

Reardon quickly removed her slacks, totally in charge now, his earlier nervousness forgotten. He pressed his cheek to her thigh, closing his eyes, and Leda watched him through her lashes, scarcely able to breathe. His skin was burning hot, the muscles in his upper arms and back rigid with tension. He got up, shedding the rest of his clothes. He returned to pull off her silken panties, gazing at her naked body with such intense longing that Leda curled up on the bed, turning away from him, suddenly shy.

Reardon dropped next to her, enfolding her tenderly, stroking her until she relaxed.

"What is it?" he said quietly. "Am I scaring you? I don't mean to, it's just that you're so beautiful, and it's been so long."

"It has for me too," Leda whispered, nestling into his strong body, comforted by his gentleness.

"What do you mean?" he asked, his tone muffled, uncomprehending.

"I only had one lover before you, and that was years ago." She closed her eyes and buried her face on his bare shoulder, inhaling the clean scent of his skin. "You're not the only one who's a little out of practice," she mumbled.

"Leda. Baby, why didn't you tell me?" he said, running his hands down the satiny curve of her back. When she didn't answer, he went on. "And I was worried that I wouldn't measure up. We're quite a pair, aren't we?"

"I think we're a wonderful pair," Leda said quickly, turning her face up to his. He kissed her again, rolling her onto her back.

"Who was he?" Reardon demanded, his face tight with jealousy.

"Nobody, Kyle, nobody at all."

"I'll make you forget him," he said fiercely, easing his weight on top of her.

"You already have," Leda answered, her breath catching as she felt the full impact of his bare skin next to hers.

He twined his fingers with hers and stretched her arms out, pinning her to the bed and kissing her prone body everywhere he could reach. Leda was transfixed with pleasure, unable to make a sound until he let her go to move lower, encircling her waist with his big hands. Leda gasped, holding his head and gliding her nails along his scalp as he caressed her with his mouth. Her hands traveled to his shoulders, damp with perspiration, and she tugged urgently, her fingers sliding on the slick, polished surface of his flesh.

"What?" he said, his voice so low and husky Leda could barely hear it.

"Come up here," she whispered.

He needed no further invitation. He moved up next to her and turned her to face him, as Leda clutched him tightly and twined her limbs around his. Reardon eased her under him, holding himself up on his hands, every atom of his body suspended, waiting. Leda looked into his eyes, and as he held her gaze he entered her, watching as her lashes fluttered closed in silent submission.

"I love you," he said into her ear. This was the last thing Leda heard before she stopped listening to anything except the runaway pounding of their racing hearts.

"Are you asleep?" Reardon murmured, pushing her damp hair back from her forehead.

"No way," Leda replied. "I'm too happy to sleep." She snuggled into the curve of his body, and his arm tightened around her.

"Are you warm enough?" he asked. "It's cooler here in the bedroom. Sometimes I just sack out on the couch in front of the fire."

"I'm exactly the right temperature," Leda answered contentedly, rubbing her cheek on his chest.

"Are you comfortable. There's another pillow in the closet, I could get it for you."

Leda giggled, propping herself up on one elbow and staring at him. "What are you doing, Mr. Reardon, taking inventory? I am absolutely wonderful, have never been better, and the only thing I ever wanted you to do for me you just did. Does that answer your questions?"

Reardon grinned. "And Jim Kendall told me you were a nice girl," he said, shaking his head.

Leda traced the outline of a scar on his left breast. "Did he really say that?"

"He really did. I think there's a little bit of matchmaker in Jim. He was trying, not too subtly, to convince me to go after you."

"Which you never did," Leda mourned. "I had to track you down with my plate of cookies and drag you into bed."

Reardon's expression became thoughtful. "That's because you're braver than I am, Leda."

She made a face. "What!"

"No, I mean it. I was running away, afraid to face my feelings, leaving it all up to you."

"Why?"

He shrugged, and she felt the ripple of muscle down his side as he moved. "I guess I had given up hope of

anything good ever happening to me again." He bent
to kiss the top of her head. "But tonight you've made
me feel like nothing is impossible."

"Kyle?"

"Mm?"

"How did you get this?" she asked, fingering the
lump of pinkish tissue that she had touched before.

He looked down at her hand. "Oh, that. I got into
a fight in prison, and knocked over a filing cabinet. It
toppled onto my chest and collapsed a lung. That's the
scar that was left after they inserted a breathing tube."

He said this so matter-of-factly that Leda didn't
know how to respond.

"Did you fight much in prison?" she finally said,
hoping her reaction to his explanation didn't show in
her voice.

"Not really," he answered, rubbing his hand ab-
sentmindedly over arm. "I was lucky, I guess, I didn't
have to. I'm big and I look—" He stopped, searching
for a word.

"Formidable?" Leda suggested.

He glanced down at her. "Is that what you think?"

She sat up to kiss him and he lifted his head to meet
her mouth with his. "Not anymore," she said. "But I
used to. That first day, when I saw you in the cemetery, I thought you looked stern and not too
friendly."'

"Oh," he replied, clearly unhappy with her
response.

"And very sexy," she added in a whisper, nipping
his shoulder lightly with her teeth.

"That's better," he said, and she laughed.

"Actually, I was left pretty much to myself," he
went on, and it was a moment before Leda realized he

was talking about prison again. "I had the run of the cell block where I was because I was always in and out working on the wiring and the plumbing, and so on. The warden even got a set of keys made up for me. It did not, however, include the key to the front door." His tone was heavy with bitter irony.

"Was it awful, Kyle?" Leda asked quietly.

"It wasn't good," he said with a shortness that indicated she shouldn't pursue the subject any further. Leda switched tracks. Her curiosity about him was endless.

"Kyle, before you went away, was there someone, a girl? A special girl for you?"

He nodded, and she could see the motion of his profile clearly outlined against the moonlit window behind them. "Yeah. We were about to get engaged." He made a dismissive gesture with the hand that rested along her flank. "She faded, when I got convicted, like everybody else."

"Did you love her very much?" Leda asked, almost choking on the words.

"I thought so," he responded. He pulled her deeper into his arms and rocked her bodily, like a child. "Until I met you, saddle shoes," he added gently, and Leda sighed, her happiness complete.

"And to think I almost spent this night drinking tea and watching television," she said.

He chuckled. "What? Let me guess. One of those terrible specials where they assemble a group of celebrities who've never seen one another before, and act like it?"

"No, no. They show those during the first week after Thanksgiving. *Christmas on the Slopes, Christmas in Somaliland, A Sri Lanka Christmas*. Then what are they showing on Christmas Eve? *Blondie Goes to College*."

Reardon laughed with her, and then said, "I guess the assumption is that you won't be watching television on Christmas Eve."

"Probably," Leda said thoughtfully. "But ever since my father died, it seems that is what I wind up doing."

"No more," he said huskily, hugging her tighter. "No more."

"Do you promise?" Leda asked, dropping her head to his shoulder.

"I promise."

Leda glanced out the window idly, and then sat up suddenly. "Kyle, look. It's snowing again."

The moon had disappeared behind a cover of clouds, and large, downy flakes were drifting earthward, visible in the light from the Masters' garage. The church on the corner was lit up for the midnight service, and the worshipers filed in through the open doors, past two giant evergreens that flanked the steps. These were decorated with rows of tiny lights twinkling like stars and, combined with the blaze inside the nave, seemed to bathe the arrivals in a welcoming glow.

"It looks like a Currier and Ives print," Reardon murmured, staring past Leda's head at the scene.

The clock in the tower chimed, and they listened together as it hit the twelfth and last note.

"It's Christmas," Leda said, and flung her arms around his neck. "The best Christmas I ever had."

"Oh, Leda," Reardon answered, a slight catch in his voice. "I hope you never change your mind about that."

"I never will," Leda whispered, raising her head to kiss him. He responded instantly, pulling her down to the bed.

Beyond the window the snow fell, silent witness to the lovers who, absorbed in each other, had forgotten it.

Leda was flung brutally to the floor, shocking her awake. Stunned, and groggy from sleep, she crawled backward, away from her attacker, throwing her arms up to protect her head.

Reardon jumped on top of her, pinning her to the dusty floorboards before he came fully awake and realized what he was doing. With an agonized cry he sprang back, picking her up and cradling her in his lap.

"Oh, my God, Leda, are you all right? Did I hurt you?" He closed his eyes briefly, seeking control, and then opened them again, searching her face anxiously.

Leda peered up at him in the meager dawn light, trying to understand what had happened. "I think so," she said unsteadily, rubbing the back of her head where it had hit the wooden floor. "Did you have a nightmare?"

He nodded, biting his lip. "I thought I was back in jail, and then waking up and finding someone next to me in bed..." He let it trail off, and Leda didn't say anything more. She understood.

"I can't believe I did that to you." he said, touching her face gently. Then he straightened suddenly, letting her go and slamming one fist into the other in frustration. "Do you see now why I didn't want you to get involved with me?" He pulled away from her entirely and stood up, reaching for his jeans and yanking them on. Leda scrambled after him, wrapping herself in the sheet from the bed and following him into the other room. He was sitting on the sofa with his head in his hands. When she touched his shoulder he jerked away, as if burned.

"Kyle, you didn't hurt me, I'm fine," she said quietly, sitting next to him.

"You're not fine, none of this is fine!" he responded savagely. "How can you say such a thing? This is so sordid, can't you see that? Because of what happened to me, because of where I was and what went on there, I can never be what you want. Never!"

"You're exactly what I want," Leda answered firmly. "Do you think I'm going to walk out on you because of one little incident?"

"One little incident," he repeated incredulously, staring at her. "Is that what you call it? I could have killed you, don't you understand that?"

"Don't be ridiculous, Kyle. There's not a mark on me. I've fallen before, and I will again. You were hurt worse when you lost that battle with the Fiat's fender this morning," she said, touching the patch of gauze on his forehead, trying to joke him out of it.

"You didn't *fall*, you were thrown," he said grimly. He stood up and paced back and forth like a caged animal, then stopped and faced her. "What if it happens again?" he asked her.

"It won't, darling," Leda said, getting up and going to him. She sighed with relief when he didn't pull away and accepted her embrace. "It's just the newness of this," she added soothingly, stroking his hair. "Once you get used to me being with you, you'll adjust."

"Aren't you afraid now?" he asked, his voice close to breaking. "Leda, I don't want you to be afraid of me."

Leda pulled back and looked up into his face. His beautiful eyes were wet with unshed tears.

"You asked me that once before," she answered, putting her finger against his lips. He kissed it. "I wasn't then, and I'm not now. I don't know why, but nothing anyone said about you could alter what I felt in my heart. And what happened this morning doesn't change anything either." She rubbed her fingertip over his mouth, and he closed his eyes. "I didn't expect you to be perfect, Kyle. No one is. I know you'll have problems fitting back into daily life, but I'll help you with them. We'll face them together, okay?"

"Okay," he answered hoarsely, hugging her tightly. Then he released her and turned away, wiping the back of his arm across his eyes. "I'll get you the blanket, and start another fire," he said briskly, obviously trying to disguise his pain by concentrating on mundane matters. Leda let him fuss over her, bundling into the blanket he brought from the bed and watching as he built a new fire.

"I'll make some coffee too," he added as he pulled the firescreen across the open hearth.

"Now, there I draw the line," Leda announced, getting up and putting her arms around his waist from behind. He smelled of warmth, and sleep, and her.

"You make terrible coffee," she whispered into his ear, and he turned to grin at her as she made her way to the kitchenette, trailing her makeshift robe behind her.

It's Christmas Day, Leda thought as she rinsed the pot under the tap. And I certainly got what I wanted for Christmas.

Seven

I hate to leave you alone," Leda said at the door as Reardon helped her on with her coat.

"Forget it, Leda. I know you have to go to your aunt's house."

"But it's Christmas."

"It's just another day to me. I'm always alone, I'm used to it. Go on, now. I'll meet you at your place later."

"What time?" Leda asked, fingering the collar of his shirt.

He shrugged. "You tell me."

"Let me see. I'll get away as fast as I can. How does six o'clock sound?"

"Great. I'll be there."

Leda squinted through the door as he opened it, trying to see if anyone was outside. She hesitated, peering down the block. The morning sunlight was blinding.

"What's the matter with you?" Reardon asked. "You're acting like you're under surveillance by the FBI."

"Almost. Sara Master is probably crouched behind her curtains with a telescope."

He grinned. "Don't be ridiculous. I'm a very dull tenant. If the old lady has been counting on me for entertainment, she's been terribly disappointed."

"I wouldn't say that," Leda responded archly. "Do you know she's been monitoring the return addresses on your mail and reporting on them to my aunt Monica?"

He pulled her back inside and shut the door. "What did you say?"

"You heard me," Leda said, rearranging the scarf he had used as a lever. "Do you think I'm exaggerating now? If she sees me hotfooting it out of here, it will be all over Yardley by tomorrow."

Reardon's face closed and he turned away. "I see. And you wouldn't want anyone to know you were socializing with the criminal element, right?"

Leda moved around him to make him face her. "How can you say that to the woman who kissed you in front of the entire crew of Phelps Aircraft not one month ago? I'm merely trying to avoid trouble for you, Kyle. You've had enough to deal with already." She touched his arm, smiling at him. "I want to tell my aunt about us myself first, that's all."

He regarded her seriously. "What are you going to say?"

"I don't know. I have to think about it. But I want you to take me to the New Year's Eve bash at the country club, so it will have to be in the next few days. Her charity group is sponsoring the party."

Reardon's mouth opened. No sound emerged.

"What's wrong, Kyle? Cat got your tongue?"

"Leda, you've lost your mind. I can't take you to some fancy party with all your aunt's friends. She'll kill me, and then commit you to a mental institution."

"No, she won't. She'll accept the situation, and you, because she has to."

"So that's your plan to put me on the road to reinstatement? Drag me along to this shindig so you can force your ex-con boyfriend down everybody's throats? Swell idea, Leda. That's going to make both of us real popular."

"Well, what do you suggest?" Leda countered. "Sneaking around in back alleys under cover of night, until somebody finds out anyway? We have nothing to be ashamed of, and I refuse to act as if we do. Now, I already promised my aunt I would go to this party, and I'm not going to bring anyone else but you. Is that clear?"

"It's clear, all right," he said, unconvinced. "Stupid, but very clear."

"Kyle," Leda said gently, "I can't take time to fight about this now, I'm late already. I have a ton of presents to wrap, and I told Monica I'd be there before noon to help with the dinner. I'll see you at my place at six, okay?"

He eyed her warily, his expression dubious.

"Okay?" she repeated, louder.

"Okay, saddle shoes," he finally conceded, bending to kiss her. "It's your family," he added, straightening and opening the door again.

Leda smiled at him broadly, proud of herself for winning the point. She breezed through the doorway out to the porch.

"Look out for Sara," Reardon hissed in a dramatic stage whisper. "She may have the driveway bugged." He shut the door with a bang.

It's entirely possible, Leda thought, muttering to herself as she made her way through the soft new snow to the street. She glanced back at the house as she reached the curb. The empty windows of the first floor stared back at her. Leda's eyes moved higher and she saw Kyle standing at his window, watching her departure. He lifted his hand in farewell, and Leda walked on.

Her car, when she reached it, was frosted with two inches of snow. Leda got the brush out of the trunk and cleared it off, spraying the glass with deicer to improve visibility. She paused in her labors to inspect the damage to her fender, which looked no worse than it had the previous night. Leda got in and turned the key in the ignition, wondering if it would start. She hoped the cold hadn't killed the battery. It turned over on the first try, however, and she drove back to her apartment, thinking about the marvelous changes that had taken place since she was last in the driver's seat.

When she got back to her house she hurried inside and showered quickly, changing into the green velvet dress she had purchased to wear for the holiday. She wrapped her remaining gifts and checked the messages on her answering machine. There were two: one from Chip, restating his plea for her to attend Anna's party, and the other from Monica, reminding her bring her mother's punch bowl set to dinner. The first required no action, since the party was over and she hadn't gone, but she groaned when she heard the second one. Leda had forgotten about the punch bowl, which was on the top shelf of the kitchen cupboard, accessible only to giants and normal human beings standing on step ladders. She dragged the ladder to the closet and retrieved the set piece by piece, until she had assembled the whole thing. Then she packed all the parts in a cardboard box, carefully wrapping the tiny cups and the ladle in tissue paper. She taped the box shut and glanced at the clock. Damn. Monica would be tapping her foot in the entry hall, one eye on her watch. She revered punctuality the way the Borgias had revered power, and Leda wanted to keep her aunt in a good mood. Leda grabbed her burdens and fled, buttoning her coat as she raced out the door. She had to make two trips to the car until she had everything stowed inside it, and then drove off, feeling like Kriss Kringle getting a late start from the North Pole.

Leda was, of course, the last to arrive. Her cousin Martha answered the door, making a jovial comment about the person who lived closest always showing up late, and Leda smiled weakly, handing her the punch bowl. The rest of the relatives were in the living room with Uncle Matt, the brother of Monica's late husband, who was telling a story about his days on the Boston police force. Leda went quietly into the kitchen, depositing her burdens on the way. Cousin Martha trailed in her wake.

"It's about time," Monica greeted her, turning from the stove.

Leda sighed. "Merry Christmas, Aunt," she said, going to kiss Monica on the cheek. "I brought the punch bowl set," she added, gesturing to Martha.

"Good," Monica replied, nodding. "The egg nog is in the refrigerator. You girls get started on that and take it into the others. Then, Leda, I want you to come back out here and help me with this soup."

Leda and Martha exchanged glances. It was clear that Monica was well into her annual holiday fooda-thon, during which she produced all her standard del-icacies on a rotating basis, complete with orders for distribution and consumption. Leda and Martha si-lently set up the punch bowl and took it into the liv-ing room, where they were greeted by a chorus of cheers. The celebration was under way.

Christmas was the longest day of Leda's life. She usually enjoyed the holiday, but every time she thought of Reardon waiting for her at home, she wanted to ditch the family scene and bolt out the front door. But she stuck it out to a decent hour, and was rewarded by the comments of several of her relatives, who told her how well she was looking. Her night with Reardon was showing. Uncle Matt even told her that a theatrical career must be agreeing with her, because she seemed very happy. Leda smiled to herself. That she was.

She lasted through coffee and dessert, and the opening of the gifts, before she started making noises about leaving at five-thirty. She endured the standard protests, saying that she had work to do at home, which led to speculation about what that work might be, since everybody knew all actresses had to do was look pretty for the audience. Such comments usually irritated her, but she was in such a transcendent mood that she nodded and smiled, edging ever closer to the door. She finally departed at ten minutes to six, amidst a flurry of hugs and kisses and promises to keep in touch. She was richer by an assortment of gloves and scarves and books, as well as a cashmere sweater from Monica, which Leda had admired while shopping with her aunt but dismissed as too expensive. Leda felt guilty about her comments to Kyle concerning her aunt. Monica loved her, and was doing her best, which was all anyone could do.

Leda forced herself to drive slowly back to her apartment. She wanted to race through the snow-laden street, screeching around corners on two tires, but she also wanted to live to see Kyle again, so she took her time. It seemed an eternity before she pulled up in front of her house.

The street was empty, without another car in sight. Leda swallowed her disappointment as she walked up to her door. Kyle must be late. She got out her keys, wondering where he was.

A figure stepped out of the shadows, and she jumped, dropping her key ring into the snow. Reardon caught her against his chest, laughing softly.

"I told you I'd be here," he said into her ear. "Who did you think it was?"

"I didn't see a car," she responded, hugging him and closing her eyes. "You scared me."

"I'm sorry," he said, letting her go and bending to retrieve her keys. He dusted them off and unlocked the door. "I told you I like to walk in the cold." He pushed open the door and hustled her inside. "But tonight I had enough of it." He pulled her into his arms again. "I missed you," he said huskily.

"I missed you too," Leda said into his shoulder. "I wish that you could have been with me, but showing up with you on my arm would have been too much for Monica's heart. I have to break it to her gently."

"That ought to be a good trick," Reardon said dully, releasing Leda and watching as she took off her coat.

"Now, don't get started on that again," Leda replied, a warning in her tone.

He shrugged. "All right. But I can understand how he feels. If you were my niece I'd steer you off somebody like me." He looked around the room. "This is nice," he said. "Quite a change from the Reardon Arms."

Leda glanced at his face. He wore the closed expression that meant he was unhappy.

"I don't care where you live," she whispered, throwing her arms around his neck and almost knocking him off-balance. "I love you, I love you, I love you. Got the picture?"

He relaxed, and she could feel the tension leave his body as it enfolded hers. "I've got the picture," he said. He held her off and examined her from head to foot. "You look beautiful."

She pirouetted for him. "Thank you. I should. This dress is a sample I modeled in a show, and I was able to buy it for half price. Otherwise I wouldn't be wearing it."

He looked away from her, walking thoughtfully around the room, studying objects but not picking them up, as if he were in a museum.

"Do you do that a lot?" he asked suddenly.

"What?" Leda asked, spinning around to look at him. Something in his voice concerned her.

"Model in shows, stuff like that." He gazed at her, his gunmetal eyes intent.

She shrugged. "Sometimes. Whenever I can. The money is good and often you can get a deal on the clothes. I can't do photography, I'm too heavy, but runway modeling is…'' She trailed off as she saw his gaze slide away from hers. He turned his back and walked to the other side of the room, where he stared at a picture of her father, framed on an end table. Leda followed, taking his arms and turning him around.

''Kyle, what is it? Tell me.''

He didn't answer for a moment, and then said slowly, ''I don't understand what you see in me. You're pretty, a model, and smart, you could have anybody. What the hell are you doing with me?''

Leda sighed. ''I thought we just cleared that up. What brought this on, anyway, this 'I am unworthy of Leda Bradshaw' routine? It's boring, Kyle.''

''It's nothing new,'' he answered tightly. ''I've always thought that, from the day we met. You could do a lot better than a grounded pilot with a prison record.''

''Wait a minute,'' Leda said, holding up her forefinger. ''I know what this is. You sat around all day thinking about me with my family, and how if you were somebody else I could have brought you with me, and you convinced yourself that my involvement with you was going to ruin my life. Close?''

''It *will* ruin your life,'' he responded. ''If I can't get my act together I'm going to be a mechanic scraping by on the good will of kindhearted old Jim Kendall. And if he ever moves on, I have no doubt I'll be out on my ear the same day.''

''So you'll be a mechanic,'' Leda said. ''And there is a world beyond Yardley. We can go anywhere if it doesn't work out at Phelps. What is going on, Kyle, are you trying to tell me you've had second thoughts about last night?''

He dropped his eyes. "Last night was the best thing that has ever happened to me. I know I didn't say it then, but I felt it." He looked up. "I feel it now."

Leda put her arms around him and leaned into his body. "Then what are you babbling about, man?" she asked him, her voice quavering with relief.

He stroked her hair. "I'm afraid I won't be able to prove my innocence, and I don't want you to be tied to a convicted felon," he said simply.

"You'll prove it," she answered. "I'm going to make sure of that."

He stiffened and pulled away from her. "Wait a minute. No, you're not."

"Sure I am. We're going to get started on it right away."

"We?" he said, raising his brows. "Oh, no. Leda, this is my problem. I don't want you getting involved."

"I love you, I already am involved. Besides, you told me I could help you." She smiled up at him.

"I told you that you could help me get used to life on the outside again. We're not talking about the same thing. I don't want you mixed up in this, it could be dangerous. The guy who stole my formula isn't going to welcome any interest, and there could be a lot of money involved. That means high stakes, high risks. Do you understand?"

"I understand," she repeated meekly, careful not to promise anything.

"All right," he said, mollified. He reached into the pocket of his jacket, which he still wore, and produced a small, brightly wrapped package. "I almost forgot. This is for you." He put it into her hand.

Leda stared at it. "What is this?"

"It's a bomb, what do you think it is? Merry Christmas, saddle shoes." He kissed the top of her head.

"Kyle, everything is closed on Christmas Day," Leda said. "Where on earth did you get this?"

"Hotels are open," he answered, winking. "I drove to Princeton and got it in the gift shop at the Hyatt Regency."

"You drove to Princeton?" she repeated dumbly.

"Yes, Leda, Princeton, not Paris. I had nothing else to do, and I wanted to get you something. Now, are you going to stand there all night like a statue, or are you going to open it?"

"The Hyatt Regency," she said. "That's such an expensive place. I don't know, Kyle..."

"That's it," he sighed, snatching the box out of her hands. "I'm taking it back."

Leda lunged for it, and he laughed, holding it out of her reach.

"Now, are you going to be nice and open this without further commentary?" he asked, waving the box above his head.

"I am," she answered dutifully, folding her hands and looking at the floor.

He lowered the box, and she grabbed it, ripping off the paper greedily. He watched her, smiling slightly.

Leda lifted the cover and looked inside. On a bed of cotton wool lay a delicate necklace of thin gold links. Suspended from it was a miniature mask of comedy, the symbol of the actors' trade since ancient times, when the Greeks used it to decorate their amphitheaters.

"Turn it over," he instructed as Leda touched it with a delicate forefinger.

She did. The other side was the mask of tragedy. She lifted the chain from the box and slipped it around her neck. "It's perfect, Kyle," she said softly. "I'll never take it off."

He chuckled, hugging her and kissing her gently. "You have my permission to take it off," he said. "But only on special occasions."

"Don't tease me," she whispered. "I'm so happy. I never believed I could be this happy." She shivered suddenly. "It scares me."

"Why?" he asked, pulling a strand of hair out of her collar and running it through his fingers. "Isn't that what everyone wants, to be happy?"

"Yes, but..." She thought about it. "I have 'that which I fear to lose.' You know what I mean, don't you?"

"Yes," he said soberly. "Yes, I do." They embraced in silence, and then Leda tugged at his hand and led him through the kitchen to the back of the house. "There's my tree," she said proudly, pointing through the glass door to the porch. "What do you think?"

He surveyed it appraisingly. "I don't know. Couldn't you have gotten a bigger one?"

"Very funny," Leda replied. "You should join forces with Claire. She said it belonged in Rockefeller Center."

Reardon nodded, agreeing. "Either there, or on the south lawn of the White House."

"You're just jealous," Leda said airily.

He grabbed her and nuzzled her neck, running his hands over the smooth surface of her dress. "Who's Claire?" he asked, his voice muffled by the soft curve of her exposed shoulder. "And where's the bedroom?"

"Claire is my friend who lives next door," Leda answered, her eyes closing. "And the bedroom is right down the hall from the living room."

"You'd better show me," he said huskily. "It's hard to find your way around in a new place."

Leda turned and they walked hand-in-hand to the door.

"Should I carry you across the threshold?" Reardon asked, half kidding.

"I think you already did that last night," Leda replied.

"Oh, right," he said, snapping his fingers. "I was wondering how I wrenched my back."

She threw him a dirty look, and he responded by snatching her off her feet and hoisting her over his shoulder in a fireman's carry. Leda squealed in protest, laughing, as he strode into the room and tumbled her gently to the bed. Before she could move he dropped on top of her, holding himself up on his hands.

"You're crushing my new dress," she pointed out, not caring at all.

"I guess I'll have to take it off," he replied solemnly, sitting up and lifting her with him. She raised her arms as he pulled the drop-waist shift over her head and threw it in a backward arc. It came to rest on her dresser.

"So much for that," he said, kissing the valley between her breasts exposed by her skimpy bra. He removed the rest of her underwear, caressing her slowly as he tossed the delicate items on the floor.

"Kyle?" Leda whispered, awash in sensation as he trailed his lips lightly over her belly.

"Mm?" he grunted, absorbed in his task.

"Don't you think you'd better take your jacket off?" she asked him laughing softly. His mouth moved lower, and her laughter faded. She moaned and clasped him to her, protesting when he finally stood to take off his clothes. She shifted restlessly, reaching for him.

"I'm always more interested in undressing you," he said quietly in belated reply to her question. When he stretched out beside her, she melted into him, fitting herself into the curve of his body and sighing with satisfaction. His lean, hard body was the perfect complement to her softer, rounded one, and to rest in his arms was like coming home.

"I thought about this all day," he said, pulling her tighter against him. "The minute you left I couldn't wait for you to come back, so I could touch you again. Once you were gone I became convinced I'd imagined the whole thing, probably because I *had* imagined it so many times in the past."

"Did you?" Leda asked. "So did I."

He stared at her, surprised.

"What's the matter? Don't you think ladies have fantasies like that?" Leda smiled, touching the slight cleft in his chin with the ball of her thumb. "I couldn't sleep the night after I kissed you at the hangar. The memory of it kept me awake."

"Oh, I slept all right. I dreamed. Constantly. And you were always the subject."

"Is the reality a disappointment?" Leda asked, certain of the answer but wanting to hear him say it just the same.

He kissed her deeply, murmuring against her mouth, "The reality is far superior to the dream. Is that what you had in mind?"

"Yes," she responded, raking her nails lightly down the smooth surface of his spine. He turned her fully, sliding his legs between hers. "You're carving me up," he whispered, nipping her ear. "My back looks like a relief map of Bolivia."

"Does it hurt?" she asked, concerned, trying to sit up.

"Not at all," he answered, pushing her down firmly. "And don't stop. I like to see the cool, capable Miss Bradshaw turn into a tigress in bed." He bent his head and laved her nipples with his tongue, caressing her relaxed limbs with his free hand. His touch became more intimate, and Leda writhed in frustration, finally grasping his slim hips and pulling him toward her with surprising strength.

"Kyle," she moaned, unable to say anything more than his name.

He understood, closing his eyes with pleasure as her hands found him and guided him home. He thrust into her powerfully, and Leda's head fell back as she enfolded him in the ultimate embrace.

"Sweet Leda," he said hoarsely, seeking her mouth with his. "I'll never need to dream again, as long as I have you."

Leda clung to him, falling into his rhythm, inarticulate with a surfeit of feeling she couldn't express.

We'll work it out, she thought before she ceased to think at all. We love each other, and nothing that happens now can tear us apart.

At that moment, she believed it.

Leda awoke about an hour later to the sound of suspicious noises in the kitchen. She got a robe from her closet and slipped into it, padding barefoot down the hall and pausing in the doorway. Kyle was rooting around in the refrigerator, clinking bottles and jars. His head was completely submerged inside, and he was visible only from the waist down, wearing his faded blue jeans, and loafers without socks.

"Hungry?" Leda asked, and his head appeared.

"There are nothing but condiments in here," he complained, disgusted. "What do you eat for breakfast? Relish?"

"I'm sorry the contents don't meet with your approval," Leda answered dryly. "I wasn't expecting a raid."

He slammed the door shut and confronted her, folding his arms. "I'm starving," he announced.

"So I gathered. There's a care package out in the car, which I thoughtfully assembled after dinner. It's yours for the taking if you want to brave the cold."

"I'm gone," he said, heading for the door. Leda darted into the bedroom and grabbed his jacket, running after him with it.

"Kyle, put this on. You'll freeze before you hit the street."

He shrugged into it dutifully, on his way.

"It's the shopping bag in the backseat," she called after him, listening to his progress down the steps. He returned quickly, stamping his feet.

"It must be ten degrees out there," he said, carrying the bag into the kitchen. He deposited it on the table, and Leda unloaded its contents, identifying them one by one.

"Turkey sandwiches," she announced, tossing him a foil-wrapped packet. He caught it with one hand.

"Fruitcake," she said, sending another sailing his way. He palmed it and set it beside the first one.

"Sliced ham," she said, "and, the pièce de résistance, Uncle Matt's chocolate nut surprise." He snared both in mid-air.

"What's the surprise?" he asked suspiciously, peeling open the foil on the last bundle.

"That's just the name, dummy," Leda said, exasperated. "They're brownies."

He nodded, popping one into his mouth. "Good," he pronounced.

"Uncle Matt will be so pleased," Leda answered.

"No stuffing?" Reardon asked, disappointed, peering into the empty bag.

"These are the leftovers, Kyle, not the main course."

He settled for a turkey sandwich and sat at the kitchen table, washing it down with a glass of water from the sink.

"Aren't you hungry?" he asked Leda when he realized that she was standing idle, watching him.

"I just ate a couple of hours ago," she reminded him. She walked over to him and rearranged his hair, mussed from the bed and the wind outside.

"You need a haircut," she observed.

"I always need a haircut," he answered. "My hair grown like weeds. In prison, the only person who saw the barber more often than I did was his wife."

Leda's hand fell away, and she turned from him. He reached out and caught her wrist, rising to stand beside her, the food forgotten.

"It bothers you when I talk about it, doesn't it?" he asked quietly.

"Only because you were hurt there," she replied. "I want to know about it, I want to know everything about you, but sometimes the memory of the pain is so clear in your voice that I can't bear it." She put her head against his shoulder, and he held her loosely, stroking her hair.

"Let's go back inside," he said huskily, and Leda moved with him, unable to deny him anything.

Sometime during the night she woke to find Kyle sleeping beside her, the blanket caught around his waist, his dark hair an inky stain against the pillow. She traced his shoulders lightly with a feathery touch too insubstantial to wake him. He stirred a little rolling toward her, and when he felt her next to him, he sighed and relaxed, his fingers closing around her arm. So much for the bad dreams, Leda thought. He's already getting used to having me with him. She settled the blanket more carefully around him, resolving that she was going to help him whether he wanted her to or not. And she had an idea just where to begin.

Eight

The next day Leda got up early and retrieved the boxes of her father's things that Phelps had given her. She brought them up from the cellar and spent a couple of hours going through his papers and correspondence, but it was very slow work. The containers were absolutely crammed with reams of notes and memos, file folders and ledgers, and eyestrain finally forced her to stop. Much of the written material was in her father's tiny, cramped handwriting, and took concentration to interpret. If she had had any grandiose ideas about coming up with evidence to clear Reardon from a quick perusal of this stuff, she now knew that she was sadly mistaken. Leda put aside the boxes reluctantly, carefully segregating the material she'd already covered. She'd get back to the task as soon as she could.

She changed clothes for the matinee at the playhouse, and then called her agent. She wanted to see if she could reschedule the audition that she missed on Christmas Eve. She learned that it was too late, the job was gone. Leda sighed heavily, about to hang up, when her agent interrupted with news of a theatrical tour slated to begin a few days after the end of her run at the playhouse. It was a Shakesperean company looking for an actress capable of playing an ingenue as well as the full range of other roles, and they wanted to see Leda. Leda turned her agent down flat, something she would not have believed possible a few months before, when her career was the consuming interest in her life. She had no intention of traveling the country, even if it was a chance to work in repertory, performing the brainchildren of her favorite playwright. She was with Reardon now, and she wasn't going anywhere.

Just before Leda left to go to work she put in a call to John Caldwell, her father's lawyer, who also handled her legal matters. When he returned it, she intended to ask him for all the information he had on her father's company, and its connection to Reardon's trial.

She hung up with a satisfied smile.

Kyle didn't know it, but help was on the way.

Reardon awoke and reached for Leda. With his eyes still closed, his seeking hand came up empty, and it was a couple of seconds before he opened them and realized that she was gone. He was back in his apartment, she was doing a matinee, and he had the 3-11 shift at Phelps.

He rolled over and glanced at the clock—one-thirty. He closed his eyes again and thought about Leda. Memories of their lovemaking washing over him, and his fingers curled into the sheets, his stomach tightening. Then he jumped up, throwing off the blanket, shaking his head. Enough of that. He would save it for the lady herself when he saw her later.

Reardon zipped up his jeans and walked out to the kitchen. He made coffee, using the method Leda had shown him, which yielded marvelously improved results. As he crossed to the cabinet he saw her pocket mirror lying on the kitchen table where she had left it. He picked it up, turning it over to look at himself, unable to restrain a smile.

She found him handsome, she wanted him, she loved him.

"Reardon," he said to the image in the glass, "I think your luck has finally changed."

Leda and Reardon spent the next several days together, snatching every moment they could from their work schedules to make up for lost time, They went skiing on Reardon's day off, which proved enjoyable for him, but Leda spent most of her hours on the slope flat on the ground, soaking wet. She hadn't been skiing since high school, and even as a teenager she had never threatened to be an Olympic contender. Reardon found her spills and wildly uncontrolled runs vastly amusing, until he tried to help her and she pulled both of them into a fence. He disentangled her rented skis from the wire mesh barrier, with the aid of a patrol guide, and readily agreed when the guide suggested that maybe they'd better call it a day. On the way home they stopped at a restaurant for dinner, and wound up checking into the attached hotel when they couldn't wait to make love until they got back to Yardley.

Leda had never been so happy. She took Reardon to New York to see a play, and was surprised and delighted when his comments afterward indicated an understanding of her craft not shared by many laymen. He also wanted to go ice skating, but Leda balked at the suggestion, pleading that they do something not connected in any way with snow or ice. They went roller skating instead, and she managed to stay on her feet, but just barely. She didn't share his enthusiasm for athletic pursuits, but he seemed unfazed by her clumsiness, tolerantly correcting her mistakes, and she actually began to improve.

They spent an inordinate amount of time in bed. When Leda teased him that he was trying to make up for four years of abstinence in a single week, he admitted it instantly and pulled her back under the covers again.

Finally, on the day before New Year's Eve, when Leda knew she could avoid it no longer, she went to see her aunt.

Monica opened the door to let her in, remarking that she thought Leda had vanished off the face of the earth.

"I've been busy," Leda answered, taking off her coat and following her aunt into the kitchen, where she was chopping vegetables for soup.

"I guess so," Monica said. "Martha told me she left three messages on your machine about your visiting them in Wynnewood, and you never called her back."

"I'll call her today," Leda responded guiltily. She'd been avoiding her whole family over the holiday season, unwilling to answer questions about her love life or the man she'd been seeing. But the showdown was at hand, and she knew it.

"When is your last performance at the play-house?" Monica asked, attacking a stalk of celery with a cleaver.

"Sunday."

"What will you do then?"

"Go to the wrap party the director is throwing for the cast," Leda replied, grinning.

Monica looked up from the cutting board and fixed her with a deadly glance. "You know that isn't what I meant. What will you do for a *job*?"

"I'll continue to try out for parts, just like I did before I got this one. We've had this conversation before, Monica. I don't know why you think I'm suddenly going to announce I'm accepting a position with a bank, or something. This is my choice, and I'm going to stick with it."

Monica chopped in silence, her mouth grim.

"Speaking of choices," Leda said casually, "there's something else I have to tell you."

Monica looked up, her gaze inquiring.

"Do you remember when we ran into Kyle Reardon at the cemetery, and then I came across him a few days later, at Phelps?"

Monica put down the knife and turned to Leda, who now had her full attention.

"Of course I remember," Monica responded cautiously. "I remember how I tried to talk to you about it, and the reception I got. Don't tell me this has something more to do with that man."

"Yes," Leda said, and waited.

"You haven't been seeing him," Monica said, almost certain of the answer.

"Yes, I have."

Monica nodded. "I knew you wouldn't listen to me, you never do. Well, out with it. Do you want to bring him over here for dinner, or some crazy idea like that? I'm warning you Leda, that criminal will never be a guest in this house, so if that's what you're thinking, you can just drop it right now."

"I don't want to bring him here for dinner," Leda said evenly. "I'm going to bring him to the country club for the New Year's Eve party, and I wanted you to know in advance."

Monica pulled out a chair and sank into it, her face gray. It was several seconds before she could manage to speak.

"This is a joke," she whispered.

Leda faced her calmly. "Do I look like I'm kidding?"

"Why would you do a thing like that to me?" Monica asked.

"I'm not doing anything to you," Leda said gently, going to her aunt and touching her arm. Monica yanked it away.

"Well, what would you call it? I'll be a laughing stock in front of my friends."

"No, you won't," Leda answered cheerfully. "I will. And I don't care. I love Kyle and I want everyone to see that I don't hold him responsible for what happened to my father."

"You love him," Monica repeated, closing her eyes.

"That's right."

"Oh, my God," Monica whispered. "All I can say is I'm glad your father didn't live to see this. In fact, your lover is the reason he didn't live to see anything." She put the back of her hand to her forehead, rubbing it.

"Don't ever say that again," Leda responded tightly. "It isn't true."

Monica laughed mirthlessly. "Isn't it? You're a fool, Leda. You have always been just like your mother, romantic and wildly impractical. Oh, you act like a goal-oriented career woman, you spout that jargon with the best of them, but when it comes right down to it, you're as full of dreams as Sleeping Beauty. First it was this nonsense about being an actress, and now this liaison with the man who as good as killed your father." She shook her head, shrugging helplessly.

"Kyle, didn't do anything wrong. He was convicted for a crime he didn't commit."

"Oh, I'm sure that's what he is telling you."

"I believe him."

Monica looked at her niece earnestly. "Leda can't you see that this man is using you? He wants you to show him around to regain his lost status in this town. Everybody knows he wants to make points for the reinstatement of his license. How could anyone fail to believe his story when the daughter of the man he supposedly ruined obviously accepts his innocence?"

Leda looked away uncomfortably. "It was my idea to bring him to the party. He doesn't want to go."

"Did he object very strenuously?" Monica asked sarcastically. She stood and put her palm on Leda's shoulder. "Darling, you're playing right into his hands."

Leda moved out of her aunt's reach. "I can see where you would feel that way. But you're wrong. I know him better than anyone, and I know he's innocent.''

Monica saw that she wasn't getting through and tried another tack. ''How can you be sure you know him so well? You only met him a short time ago.''

''The amount of time I've known him is irrelevant. He's good—''

''In bed?'' Monica interrupted cuttingly.

Leda stared at her angrily. ''I don't deserve that.''

''I think you do. I think you're being influenced by the man's undeniable attractiveness. I've seen him, Leda. I may be old, but I'm not dead. Don't you think I know how a man like that can work his way with you, play with your affections until you don't know which end is up? I've seen it happen many times before. You wouldn't be the first, believe me.''

''And how are you so sure he's guilty?'' Leda countered. ''Suddenly you're omniscient, you know everything?''

''I was around during his trial, child, you weren't. You're not qualified to offer an opinion on what happened then, you were at school, in pigtails and flannel skirts, when it all happened.''

''I'm not at school anymore,'' Leda answered stubbornly. ''I'm all grown up now, Monica, and capable of forming my own judgments.''

''Capable of falling in love with a louse too, Leda,'' her aunt said softly.

''He isn't a louse,'' Leda answered, trying to keep the incipient tears out of her voice. ''He's a wonderful man who got a bad break that no one will let him forget.''

''No one but you.''

''That's right. I'm going to help him.''

Monica sighed. "And how do you propose to do that?"

"I've already gotten Daddy's records from the last few months he had the company, and I'm going through them. And I've asked John Caldwell to send me his material on the trial. I'll find something that will vindicate him, I know I will."

"And what if you find something that incriminates him?"

"I won't."

Monica threw up her hands. "It's impossible to talk sense to you, you're completely out of reach. Do you actually think you're going to find something his defense attorney missed? Don't you think that if there was anything that could help him, it would have been discovered at the time of his trial?"

"Kyle says his defense attorney was in on it, that he worked with a former colleague of Kyle's to steal his formula. He made sure that he went to jail, and then went off to California with the plans."

Monica eyed her incredulously. "And you believe that?"

"Yes, I do."

"Then I give up," Monica said coldly, turning away. "I have nothing more to say."

"You could say that you'll be polite to him at the party," Leda said pleadingly. "It would mean so much to me."

"I don't understand why you insist on bringing him, but if you do, I won't be rude to him. I'm never rude to anybody, regardless of what my private opinion of them is."

"Thank you," Leda said humbly. "I would appreciate that." She turned to go. "I would also appreciate it if you would try to understand how I feel. I have to believe in him, the way I would believe in anyone I trusted. I love him, but I also like him. He's my friend."

Monica faced her, her eyes wet. "*I'm* your friend, Leda. I've been your friend for twenty-five years, since the day you were born. I've always tried to look after you for my dear sister's sake, and that's all I'm trying to do now."

Leda went to her and embraced her, kissing her cheek. "I know that, Monica, and I love you for it. But it's my life, and I have to do what I think best with it." She pulled back and looked at the older woman fondly. "I'll see you tomorrow night, then."

Monica nodded dully.

"Good-bye," Leda said and left, before Monica could call her back.

The records from the lawyer were waiting for her when she got home. Reardon was working, and Leda spent the rest of the day reading a copy of the trial transcript, including the testimony of co-workers who talked about Reardon's behavior before the disastrous test that killed the onlookers. The picture that emerged was the one that got Reardon convicted, a portrait of a headstrong, reckless experimenter who wouldn't listen to the advice of cooler, wiser heads. Leda could readily see how a jury would have been led astray by it, especially when the defense could offer almost nothing to controvert it. Those judging Reardon had believed that when he was denied permission to run the test, he had disobeyed orders and run it anyway, resulting in the fatal explosion.

Leda sighed and put the transcript aside. Kyle was

due in a few minutes, and she had to start dinner.
After the party she would go back to her father's
things and look again.

New Year's Eve was overcast and cold, a typical
winter's day. Claire called to say that she would be
driving back the next night, since she had to resume
her teaching duties on January second. Leda was unable to contain herself and told her about her relationship with Kyle, and Claire was delighted. She
wished her luck with a cautionary note about her plans
for that evening. Leda agreed not to unduly antago-
nize the locals, and hung up in good spirits, convinced that there was at least one person on her side.

Anna dropped by in the afternoon with a prop dress
Leda had gotten permission to wear for the evening.
Anna had a date with a musician from the orchestra
of a Broadway show she had appeared in, and brought
along her gown to show Leda.

"What do you think?" she asked, striking a pose
after Leda had zipped her up.

"Dynamite," Leda pronounced, nodding. "He'll
propose tonight."

"I hope not," Anna sighed, backing up so that
Leda could unzip her again. "On what the musician's
union pays him, he can barely afford to feed his cat."

"Where are you going?"

Anna shrugged. "To the apartment of some friend
of his. The guy plays the trombone, does weddings
and party gigs on weekends." She peered at Leda.
"How about you? All set for the big night?"

"I don't know. I think I'm getting cold feet. It
seemed like a great idea before, but now that the time
is at hand I'm not so sure."

"How does Kyle feel?"

"He thinks the whole project is questionable, but he's going to please me."

Anna sighed dramatically. "What a hunk. I wish he were interested in pleasing me, I'd have a few thoughts for him."

"That reminds me, I have to pick up his tux," Leda said. They both headed for the door, and Anna asked as she picked up her dress, "Did you really turn down the tryout for that touring company? Bob said you did."

Bob was Anna's agent, and a friend of Leda's agent, who worked for the same theatrical booking concern. "Yes. I didn't want to leave Kyle."

Anna raised her brows. "Well, I can understand that, but it's a great opportunity. I'm going to see them."

"Good," Leda said sincerely, locking the door behind them. "I hope you get it."

"There's room enough for two if you change your mind," Anna called over her shoulder as she went down the walk to her car.

Leda waved in reply. She wouldn't be changing her mind.

Leda was getting dressed when Kyle returned to her apartment from work. He entered her bedroom in his coveralls and held her off laughing, when she tried to kiss him.

"Leda, I'm filthy," he said.

"Has that ever been known to stop me?" she asked, winding her arms around his neck.

"No," he replied, giving in and kissing her back, peeling the robe off her shoulders.

"You're early," she said as his lips trailed over the creamy expanse of her skin.

"I told you there was split shift tonight. Everybody wants to party, including me." He backed her toward the bed.

"I picked up your tux," she informed him.

He groaned and released her. "Do I really have to wear a monkey suit to this shindig?"

"Yes, you do. This is a formal affair."

"Can't we just stay here and have our own informal affair in your bed?" he inquired, reaching for her again.

Leda danced away, smiling. "You, Mr. Reardon, have a one-track mind."

"Leda, I'm serious. Maybe we'd better skip this. It's just going to make everyone uncomfortable."

"I don't care," Leda said stubbornly. "I want all of those righteous people who've been giving you such a hard time to see me with you. Maybe they'll think twice about their high-and-mighty attitude."

"And you have an idea that if the accused escorts the daughter of Carter Bradshaw, they'll do that?"

"I hope so."

He pulled her into his arms and stroked her hair. "Leda, that's not going to make the board in Harrisburg give me my license back," he said gently.

"I know that. But I also know that part of their investigation is to question the employer and the neighbors of the person under consideration for reinstatement. Won't it help if everybody says you've been forgiven by the family of the dead man?"

"I haven't been forgiven by all of it," he said flatly, his grip loosening.

"Don't worry about Aunt Monica. She'll come around." Leda stepped out of the circle of his arms and went to her closet. "Help me into my dress," she said, holding it up for his examination.

"I'd rather help you out of your dress," he replied, but took it from her obediently, dropping it over her head and zipping it up to the waist. The silver lamé sheath left her back and one shoulder bare. He planted a lingering kiss on her spine before she turned to face him and then whistled when he saw the full effect.

"Miss Bradshaw, you're a knockout," he said gravely.

"I guess you like it."

"I sure do."

"It isn't mine."

He grinned. "Whose is it? Claire's?"

"Heavens, no. Claire's tasted run more to asymmetrical stripes in primary colors. I saw this in the prop department at the theater, left over from a production last year. I tried it on and it fit, so I asked the director if I could borrow it just for tonight."

Reardon shook his head, marveling. "You certainly have some ingenious methods for assembling a wardrobe."

"Thank you," Leda said, bowing. "With my limited finances, I have to be creative. Now for the pièce de résistance." She went back to the closet and returned with the tux, neatly assembled on a two-tier hanger and covered by a plastic bag. He eyes it suspiciously.

"Don't look like that, Kyle. It's not going to bite you."

"You sure about that?" He took it from her and examined the carefully pressed garments. "I hate these things," he muttered. "Before I went to jail I was always forced to wear one for some damn party or other. They make me feel like the dressed pig at a luau."

Leda burst out laughing. "Kyle, what an awful thing to say. I can't understand your attitude." She ran a practiced eye deliberately over his form from head to toe. "You have the perfect body for one," she pronounced. "Tall and slim and elegant." She smiled, batting her eyelashes.

He shot her an arch glance. "Flattery will get you everywhere."

"I thought so. Come on, Kyle. You'll look wonderful."

"I'll look the way I'll feel, like a damn fool." But he pulled off the plastic cover and inspected the suit more closely. "Blue?" he said, fingering the ruffled shirt.

"Of course blue. It'll be great with your eyes."

He made a face.

"Trust me," she whispered.

He smiled dryly. "Okay, Leda. This is your show. I'll go take a shower."

He ambled off down the hall, and Leda sat down to put on her makeup. Reardon returned a few minutes later, dripping, with a towel wrapped around his waist. He stood by the side of the bed, pushing back his wet hair with his palms. Leda caught sight of him in her mirror, and her breath stopped in her throat. How beautiful he was. She got up and went to him, putting her arms around him and licking the droplets that spangled his muscular arms.

"What are you doing?" he asked huskily, closing his eyes. His hand came up to the back of her head, binding her to him.

"Drying you off," she replied.

"More like turning me on." He embraced her fully, turning her toward the bed. Leda pulled back.

"Kyle, we can't. We'll be late."

"We won't be late, we won't go," he answered, reaching for the zipper on her dress.

Leda resisted. "Kyle, it's important that we go. Important for you. Now come on and get dressed, or we'll never make it out the door."

He sighed and let her go. Leda returned to her toilette, watching covertly as he put on the tuxedo. He fumbled with the studs and fussed with the cummerbund, frowning down at it as if he were trying to tie a kitchen apron around his waist.

"Oh, for heaven's sake, Kyle, let me do that," she finally said in frustration, getting up to help him. "I've never seen anybody so contrary. If you wanted to wear this thing, you'd have it on in a minute."

She adjusted the waistband and fixed the hooks at the back, patting it into place. She stood at his side as he tied the tie, and then she straightened the bow.

"There," she said. "Where's the jacket?"

He pointed, and she got it for him, helping him into it. Then they both studied his reflection in the full-length mirror. The dark material complemented his hair, and the blue shirt turned his eyes into molten silver disks.

"You're gorgeous," she breathed.

"I'm ridiculous. I look like the maître d' on a cruise ship."

"Take my word for it, every woman in the place will be transfixed. Now, are you going to stop griping and relax? I just have to brush out my hair and I'll be right with you."

Leda went back to her dressing table and unpinned her hair, letting it cascade about her shoulders. She started to brush it, and then Reardon came up behind her, taking the brush from her hand.

"I'll do that," he said softly, and she closed her eyes. He drew the brush through her thick hair until it crackled and snapped with electricity. His arms were much stronger than hers, and the result was a glowing mass of spun gold that shimmered like sunlight. She opened her eyes when he set the brush down and put her head against his shoulder.

"Will you do that for me every night?" she asked him.

"Absolutely. I have a whole list of things I'm going to do for you every night, and that will be added to it."

Leda laughed. "I think we'd better leave, Kyle," she said shakily.

"I think you're right." He got her beaver jacket and helped her into it, settling for a scarf and gloves for himself. He had no overcoat.

They took Leda's car and drove to the country club. On the way there Leda thought about the people they were likely to encounter. Unlike many other clubs of the type, Yardley's was not based on wealth, but rather the lineage of the members, many of whom could barely afford their dues. Money didn't matter, but background did, and as a result women like Elaine the seamstress and Sara Master were charter members because Elaine's ancestor founded the town and Sara's had been a circuit judge in the 1880's. Monica and Leda were accepted because Monica's father, Leda's grandfather, had been an important local lawyer with strong ties to the town blue bloods. The whole atmosphere was snobbish in the extreme, and Leda avoided the place like the plague, except when she made guest appearances to puncture the overblown self-importance of the members. She intended to do so tonight. She was already regarded as something of a renegade because of her choice of profession, and her unorthodox life-style of shuttling back and forth to New York. The other girls she'd gone to high school with were married and settled, spending their days pushing baby carts up and down the aisles of the Supermart and their summers beside the club pool. They looked upon Leda as a member of an alien species, and didn't try to conceal it. Leda smiled sardonically as they pulled up to the entrance and Reardon left the car with the attendant. The town would really have something to talk about after tonight.

The lobby of the club was spotlessly clean but a little run down; with a few exceptions, the members didn't have the capital to refurbish it. Reardon left their things with the check girl, who greeted Leda and eyed Reardon with undisguised interest.

"Hi, Greta," Leda replied. "Is my aunt here yet?"

"She's inside with the others," Greta said, smiling at Reardon.

"Thanks," Leda said dryly, taking his arm. They walked past the big Christmas tree that stood by the entrance to the main room, and over the faded Chinese carpet that had been there as long as Leda could remember.

All eyes turned toward them as they went inside. A brilliant chandelier overhead cast a white light on the buffet spread beneath it. The assembled partygoers moved back and forth from the attractively displayed food to their tables, arranged around the central dance floor. The orchestra played softly in the background, and there were a few couples dancing. Waiters circulated with trays of drinks, and Leda looked around them for her aunt. She spotted Monica, dressed in basic black and pearls, standing by the bandstand with her usual escort, the high school vice principal, a widower in his sixties.

"There she is," Leda said to Reardon, and they made their way across the room. A hush greeted their passage, and Reardon gripped her tightly.

"I feel like a hippie at a convention of Young Republicans," he whispered to her, and Leda smiled. But she could tell he was joking to cover his nervousness; these were, in effect, the people who had sent him to jail.

Monica turned to face them as they approached. Her eyes flickered over Reardon, and something registered in them, but Leda couldn't tell what it was. Her aunt's face was expressionless as she looked at Leda.

"Hello, Monica," Leda said smoothly. "I think you know Kyle Reardon. Kyle, you remember my aunt, Monica Donlon."

Kyle nodded, and Monica shook his hand stiffly, meeting his eyes briefly and then looking back at Leda. Sara Master, Elaine, and the postmistress stood in the background, riveted by the scene.

Monica introduced her escort, and after a few minutes of polite, awkward conversation, Leda said, "Kyle, I think I'd like something to drink. Shall we?"

He led her away, relieved, and got them two glasses of champagne from a passing attendant. He drew his index finger around the inside of his collar and said, "Whew. That's some tough lady. I can see where you get your grit."

"The worst is over," Leda agreed. "Look at them all staring. You'd think they had never seen two people in love before."

"That's not why they're staring, and you know it. This is probably their first close-up view of a big, bad criminal."

"Don't you believe it," Leda snorted. "Plenty of them belong in jail, but they're into the sort of white collar crime that goes unpunished, like tax evasion and illegal shelters."

Reardon grinned at her. "You really like this group, don't you?"

Leda had to laugh at that, and when the band took a break she led Kyle to the buffet table, where they helped themselves, sitting to eat in a quiet alcove away from the throng. They weren't alone long, however, before Leda saw Sara Master approaching, all smiles.

"Uh-oh," she said to Reardon. "Here comes your landlady."

He stood up when Sara stopped by the table. She greeted Leda and then turned to Reardon.

"Well, Mr. Reardon, I didn't expect to see you here."

"Why not?" Leda replied, standing between him and Sara. "I would have thought my aunt told you he was coming."

Sara flushed slightly at that but, undaunted, tried again. "This must be quite a change for you," she said to Reardon, craning her neck around Leda.

"It is," he said stiffly.

"Are you enjoying yourself?"

"Yes. It's a very nice party."

She shifted her gaze to Leda. "And what a surprise you turned out to be, young lady."

"I don't know how you can say that, Sara. You know I can always be counted on to do something unconventional."

Reardon turned away to hide his smile.

"I'm sure I don't know what you mean," Sara replied huffily. "I was unaware that you knew my tenant, that's all."

Leda nodded. "Really? I didn't think there was much about him that you missed. But then again, I wasn't sending him any mail, so how would you have guessed?"

Sara's mouth fell open, and Leda seized the opportunity to nudge Reardon toward the dance floor. They danced for a few numbers, and then he said into her ear, "Lets blow this joint. I think these people have seen enough."

"I agree," Leda said airily, and they walked together across the room and out the door. She could hear the buzz of conversation start up behind them.

"Saddle shoes," he said as he presented the ticket for her coat, "I think we pulled it off."

Leda smiled as she slipped into her jacket. "They'll be talking about this for years to come, the old fuddy-duddies."

Reardon put his arm around her. "Let's go home," he said huskily.

"Let's," Leda responded.

Back at her apartment, Reardon made love to Leda with an intensity she had not experienced before, although he had always been ardent. This was different: he seemed to be trying to posses her spiritually as well as physically, calling her name over and over, driving into her with a force that left her almost frightened. Afterward, they were both exhausted, and they drifted into sleep.

In the morning, Reardon left for Harrisburg, and another hearing on his license. He had gotten the time off from Jim Kendall, and wanted Leda to go with him. But she had her final performance to give at the playhouse, and wanted to attend the wrap party afterward, so she stayed behind. It was difficult to say good-bye to all the new friends she had made among the cast, some of whom she was sure she would never see again. Chip Caswell brought a nubile redhead to the party, who was the subject of much commentary, and Leda was happy to agree with Anna that he'd finally given up on his leading lady. Anna had signed on with the touring company, and was due to leave the next day. Leda said her farewells and left the party early, determined to have another look at her father's records.

The pile of things she had examined was growing ominously, and it had yielded nothing. She spent another fruitless evening going through some new material, and finally gave up, turning at last to a strongbox at the bottom of one of the bins. She had examined the contents once before and dismissed them: her father's wallet and keys, a lighter and half a pack of cigarettes, some other odds and ends. She took a closer look at the wallet now, and her eyes misted over when she found a picture of herself enclosed in a cellophane window, backed by a faded snapshot of her mother. She opened the billfold and found some singles, a five, and a folded sheet of notepaper. She took it out, uncreasing it idly, thinking that it was probably an old grocery list or a reminder to make a dental appointment.

It was a memo, similar to the countless others she had been perusing. She read it routinely, and then, her heart beating faster, she read it again.

From: C. Bradshaw To: K. Reardon Re: Test of B-123 fuel Under no circumstances conduct test of B-123 fuel as planned, preliminaries reveal compound to be unstable. Repeat, test is not to be conducted in my absence. Will discuss upon my return.

It was dated two days before the fatal explosion, and signed by her father.

Leda stared at the paper in her hand in stunned disbelief, and then watched as it fell to the floor.

Nine

Reardon had lied to her. He'd been lying all along. She tried to remember exactly what he'd said at the Logan Inn when she questioned him about her father forbidding the test. He had never answered her directly; instead he had launched into his sabotage story, and she'd believed him.

The truth was right under her nose. Reardon has disobeyed a direct order and killed all those people with his negligence, including, as a result, her father. He *was* responsible, and deserved to go to jail.

Leda couldn't absorb it. Why was the memo here, secreted in her father's wallet, where it was never found? Had her father sought to protect Reardon, or had Reardon hidden it? No, no, that didn't make sense. Nothing made any sense, except one clear fact: Reardon was guilty, just as everyone said.

Leda stood up abruptly, and the contents of the strongbox fell to the floor. She couldn't face Reardon, knowing this. She wouldn't do anything to get him into further trouble, but she couldn't pretend that all was the same as before either. She knew that it was cowardly, but she had to get away. And she had the perfect passport out of town—the acting company that was about to go on tour.

Wiping her streaming eyes, she called her agent and asked if she could still audition for a spot. She was told to be in New York the next morning to talk to the manager of the company, who had seen her perform at the playhouse and expressed an interest. Leda asked her agent to call him and tell him that she wanted the job. Almost as soon as she replaced the phone the manager called her back and said that she had it, if she could work out the details with him in the morning. Leda said that she could, hung up, and went straight to her bedroom to pack.

When she came back out with her suitcase, she looked around the apartment and set it on the floor. She had to leave a note for Claire. She grabbed a piece of notepaper and scribbled something about a change in plans and being unable to turn down such a wonderful chance, and stuck it through the mail slot in Claire's door. Then she called Anna and told her that she would be joining her in Atlanta the following day, where the company would already be in rehearsal. Anna was full of questions about Reardon, but Leda silenced her by saying that she would explain it all when she saw her.

That left the problem of Monica. Amazed at her own calm handling of the situation, Leda dialed her aunt's number, mentally rehearsing what she would say to her.

"Hi, it's me," Leda began when Monica answered the phone.

"I see. Fresh from your triumph at the country club?" Monica responded sourly.

Leda put her hand over her mouth for a second to stifle a sob. Then, clearing her throat, she said, "I just wanted to let you know that I'll be going out of town for a while. I just got a great offer to travel with a Shakespearean company, and I'm going to take it. The first booking is in Atlanta, and I'm going straight there. I'll call you with the information about where I'm staying, and with the rest of the itinerary, dates and places and so on. Okay?"

There was a protracted silence. Then, "Leda, tell me the truth. Is this some cover story for the fact that you're running away with that Reardon man?"

Leda closed her eyes. "No, Monica. I'm going on tour. Anna is going too, we'll be together, roommates probably."

"Kind of sudden, isn't it? You didn't say anything about this to me before."

"I just found out about it myself, and I really should jump at the chance. It's great experience."

"What about your undying love for Kyle Reardon?"

"That's all over," Leda whispered.

Monica didn't try to conceal her relief. "Well, thank God you finally came to your senses. What happened?"

"I can't talk about that now, I have to run."

"Wait a minute, Leda. A few days ago you stood in this very kitchen defending him to the death, and now you're taking off for the hills with no explanation other than 'that's all over'? You'll have to do better than that, young lady.''

"And I will, but it's too much to go into right at the moment." Leda took a deep breath, hoping that she would be able to end this conversation without her aunt suspecting how close she was to breaking down. "I'll call you as soon as I get to Atlanta. Good-bye."

Monica was calling her name as she hung up.

Leda found some tissues, blew her nose, and picked up her suitcase and purse.

When the phone began to ring again she ignored it and headed for the door. Then she paused on the threshold, looking back.

If she didn't leave Kyle some kind of message, he would come after her. He would find out where she had gone, follow her, and undoubtedly create a highly emotional scene she would rather avoid.

He would return in three days, possibly sooner when she didn't answer her phone. She had to take action to convince him to leave her alone. She got another sheet of notepaper and wrote: *I have been reading my father's records. I found the memo, and I know the truth. I'm going away on tour, please don't come after me. I'm sorry it worked out this way.*

She signed her name, barely able to see through her tears, and left the note on the kitchen table where he would be sure to find it. Then, crying uncontrollably, she grabbed up her things and ran out of the house.

The audition the next day was perfunctory, and Leda flew out of Kennedy to join Anna and the rest of the company, already in rehearsal in Atlanta.

Reardon came back to Yardley the next day, alarmed that he hadn't been able to contact Leda. When he walked into the living room of her apartment, and saw the contents of the strongbox on the floor, he knew something was dreadfully wrong. Fearing for Leda's safety, he ran from room to room and saw the half-empty closet in her bedroom and the open space where her suitcase had been. His fear turning to the dread of loss, he walked slowly back into the kitchen, where he found the note.

He read it, knowing what he was going to see before he saw it. Then he sat in a chair and folded his arms on the table before him, resting his forehead on the cushion they provided. He remained motionless for some time, enervated by despair.

Looking up, he rubbed his eyes and crushed the note he still held into a ball, throwing it across the room.

She had found the memo. He knew what that meant. He had to locate her and explain. His only thought was to get to the playhouse and ask her friends where she had gone. On the way out he checked the apartment next door, but Claire was not home. He ran back to the street and set out for New Hope.

Nobody there knew where Leda was. The director was in his office, but all he could tell Reardon was that he'd heard Leda signed on with a tour at the last minute, the same one Anna Fleming had joined. He suggested a visit to Leda's aunt. Reardon nodded wearily, thanking him. Monica Donlon was the last person on earth he wanted to see, but he was fairly sure she would know where Leda was.

He was quite a bit less sure that she would tell him.

Monica answered her door, and was shocked into silence at the sight of her visitor.

"Hello, Mrs. Donlon," Reardon said calmly. "I've been looking for Leda, and I wondered if you could tell me where she went."

"No, I couldn't," Monica replied, attempting to close the door in his face.

Reardon stuck his foot in the jamb. "It's very important that I reach her."

Monica put her hands on her hips and glared at him. "Look, Reardon, can't you see that she went out of town to get away from you? I say it's high time she saw what you are, and I thank God she finally started showing some of the sense she was born with, and gave you the gate."

"Did she tell you what happened?"

"She just said that it was over between you, and that's enough for me."

"I love her, Mrs. Donlon."

"That's your problem. Now get off my porch before I call the police."

Reardon barely had time to jump back before the door crashed shut an inch from his nose.

He sagged against the porch railing and wondered what to do. Badgering the old lady would get him nowhere; Monica was as immovable as the capitol building, and if he tried to push her any further, he probably would wind up in jail.

He could think of only one person, beside the absent Claire, who might be able to tell him something. That was John Caldwell, Carter Bradshaw's lawyer. Leda had told him that Caldwell handled her legal affairs as well. Maybe it was a shot in the dark, but it was all he had. He trudged through the snow to his car and drove down the hill into the center of Yardley.

The receptionist at Caldwell and Younger was not happy to see him. He didn't have an appointment, which upset her; her world was ruled by order, and the sight of this large, forceful-looking character lingering in the waiting room for an unscheduled interview cluttered her day. Reardon stared at her pointedly until she finally buzzed Caldwell's office and told him that a Mr. Kyle Reardon wished to see him, and could he find a moment. As Reardon had anticipated, the sound of his name was magic, and Caldwell came out to get him.

"Hello, Reardon," Caldwell said, shaking his hand. "Come inside and sit down."

Reardon followed him into the spacious office filled with sunlight, which he remembered from his days with Leda's father. He took the seat Caldwell indicated, and waited as the lawyer settled himself behind his desk.

"So," Caldwell said, "how are you?"

Reardon shrugged. "As you see me."

"You don't look any the worse for wear," Caldwell observed.

"I feel it," Reardon replied, holding the other man's gaze until Caldwell looked away.

"You got a rough deal, Kyle," Caldwell said softly. "I admit that."

"Do you?"

Caldwell spread his hands. "There was nothing anyone could do. There was no evidence, Prescott had an airtight case."

"You know he was lying, John."

Ever the cautious attorney, Caldwell said nothing.

Reardon shrugged. "It's all over now anyway, at least that part of it. That's not why I'm here."

Caldwell eyed him warily.

"Do you know where Leda Bradshaw is?"

Caldwell was startled. "What do you mean? Has she gone somewhere?"

"Apparently. I'm trying to find her. Did she say anything to you to indicate where she might go?"

"No, nothing."

"Do you know the name of her agent?"

"That's confidential information, Kyle. I can't tell you that."

"Fine. I'll go through the Equity directory one by one until I hit the right person."

"What's going on, Kyle?" Why is it so important for you to find her? I understand that you were seeing her, but..."

"How did you understand that?" Reardon asked sharply.

Caldwell looked uncomfortable. "Word gets around."

"I see. You heard about the New Year's Eve party."

Caldwell looked away. "It's a small town."

Reardon stood up. "Thanks for your time, John." He made for the door.

"I'd help if I could, Kyle," Caldwell called after him. "But I don't know anything. I really only spoke to Leda once, when she asked to see the transcript."

Reardon froze. "What transcript?"

"The transcript of your trial. She called me and wanted to get a copy of it, and I gave it to her. That's public information, you know."

Reardon closed his eyes. He knew very well what a damning picture that document presented. No wonder the memo sealed his doom. Going through the trial records had planted the subconscious seeds of doubt in her mind, and the memo had finally convinced her against him. She would never listen to him now. She wouldn't listen to him unless he got proof, and that was going to take time.

"I appreciate your seeing me, John," he said to the lawyer, turning to go.

"I'm sorry I couldn't have been of more help," Caldwell said in parting.

"Oh, you helped, John. You helped me more than you know."

Reardon closed the door of the office behind him and set off down the hall. The hell with his license, and the hell with trying to work on the case from his end. This situation called for drastic action, and he was going to take it.

He stopped at a pay phone in the lobby of the building and dialed the Phelps number. When the secretary answered, he asked to speak to Jim Kendall.

"Jim?" he said when the other man got on the line. "This is Kyle Reardon."

"You sound close. I thought you were in Harrisburg."

"I was, until this morning. Jim, listen. Can I come to your office to talk to you?"

"Sure, Kyle, what's up?"

"I have a favor to ask, and it's a big one. I'll be there in ten minutes." Reardon hung up the phone and strode purposefully toward the door.

Ten

It was spring in Boston. The frozen grip of winter had long given way to the rains of April and May, and now the Common was blooming with June abundance. Leda looked out her dressing room window at the gorgeous display, and then turned away from the sight. It should have been cheering, but it wasn't.

She hadn't heard from Reardon for six months. During that time she'd been traveling with the troupe, bringing the bard to the cities of the Eastern corridor and trying to forget the man she'd left behind in Pennsylvania. She'd had considerable success with the former endeavor, none at all with the latter.

Leda went to her mirror and glanced at her costume, routinely checking the fit. She was appearing as Kate in *The Taming of the Shrew*, and the laces of the bodice kept coming undone, which was a source of vast amusement to cast and crew. She had finally sewn in a hidden set of snaps, and they seemed to help, but she still didn't trust the blouse. The director wanted her to wear the outfit because its designer swore to its authenticity. Leda thought that if it really was authentic, the women in the sixteenth century must have led a very exciting life.

The door opened and Anna entered, carrying a stack of mail and a hatbox. She handed Leda a letter.

"For you," she said. "The concierge at the hotel sent it over."

It was from Claire. Leda opened it and learned that her tenant was engaged to her old boyfriend from Wilmington, a piece of news not guaranteed to brighten Leda's day. She was happy for Claire, of course, but during this tour she had met such an alarming array of simpletons, bores, and gigolos that she had almost decided to enter a convent. The fact that Claire was obviously doing a lot better added to Leda's general depression. There was a rent check enclosed, however, and she received it with gratitude, stowing it in her purse. She could certainly use it.

"What do you think?" Anna asked, modeling the hat she had just acquired from the wardrobe room.

It was a large chapeau, with a spray of fake ostrich plumes. Leda stared at it, speechless.

"Oh, my God," Anna said, examining herself in the mirror. "I look like Sir Walter Raleigh."

"I guess that's the idea," Leda said cautiously.

"What do you mean, that's the idea? Walter Raleigh was a man."

Leda shrugged. "Well, at least they got the period right."

Anna removed the headgear and jammed it back in the box. "They'll have to come up with something else." She stalked out of the room, muttering to herself.

Leda sighed and glanced at her watch. Dress rehearsal was at three, and the performance was scheduled for eight. She would have time for a nap in between. She was sleeping a lot lately; escape was always desirable when she had so much to forget.

For the first couple of weeks after she had left Yardley she'd been hoping to hear from Reardon, praying that she'd been mistaken and he would be able to explain it all.

But when the time passed without word, Leda realized that he had nothing to say in his defense, and gave up. Monica wrote that he had quit his job at Phelps and left town. So much for his big plans to search out the truth and make his case.

Claire had been right.

There was no case to make.

Leda dried her eyes, retied the drawstring on her blouse, and made her way down the hall to the stage.

The performance that evening went well, and Leda was pleasantly tired when she got back to her dressing room. She showered in the adjoining bathroom—the facilities were far superior to those in Bucks County— and changed to jeans and a soft sweater. Anna was off somewhere, romancing a stagehand, and Leda was drifting into a doze on the couch when there was a knock at her door.

"Come in," she called, thinking that it was the prop mistress with Anna's latest hat.

The door opened, and Reardon walked through it.

Leda sat up, instantly wide awake. Her eyes locked with his, and she felt a falling sensation in the pit of her stomach. Unconsciously her hand sought the armrest for support, as if she were bracing for an impact.

"Hello, saddle shoes," he said.

He looked wonderful. He was wearing tan chinos with a light blue shirt and a navy blue sweater, the clothes emphasizing his graceful, athletic body. His hair was shorter than she remembered it, clipped close to his head on the sides and in the front. But his gaze was the same: steady, penetrating, unnerving. Time had done nothing to diminish his power over her, and as Leda looked back at him she knew she had to be firm, or she would be tossed into the whirlpool all over again.

"Hello, Kyle," she said with an approximation of calmness.

"How have you been?" he asked, his gray eyes watchful.

"Fine."

"I was in the audience tonight. You were wonderful, you really brought Katharina to life."

"Thank you."

"I told you that you should stick with it. It looks like you made the right decision."

Leda stood up. "Yes, it does. Look, Kyle, I don't want to be rude, but we really have nothing to say to each other. I broke it off between us six months ago, for good, and I still feel the same way. So no more chitchat, okay? Get to the point. What do you want?"

He folded his arms and nodded. "All right. No more chitchat. I want you to be my wife."

Leda stared at him, stunned into silence for a moment. Then she said, "You're insane. In the first place, I wouldn't marry you if you were the last man on earth, after what you did. And in the second place, half a year has passed. Where do you get the arrogance to assume that nothing has happened to me, that I'm not married, or anything?"

"I know you're not married, or anything," he replied quietly.

"How do you know?" she demanded.

He waited a moment before saying, "I've been in touch with Anna."

Leda blinked. "You've been in touch with Anna," she repeated, in a whisper. Then, louder. "You don't even know Anna!"

"I do now."

Leda put her hands to her temples and closed her eyes. Then she opened them. "I think you'd better tell me all about it," she said with a steadiness she didn't feel.

He shrugged. "I saw her name on the playbill from Bucks County, and I knew that you and she had joined the same troupe. So I wrote to her."

"Why didn't you to write to *me*?" Leda yelled.

"Because I knew you wouldn't listen to me. But Anna wasn't emotionally involved, and I convinced her to let me know how you were doing periodically, so I could keep up with your life."

"Why that sneaking, conniving...reporting on me behind my back. Wait until I get my hands on her."

"Don't blame Anna. I couldn't take the chance that you might get involved with someone else before I had the opportunity to give you this." He took a piece of paper from his pocket and handed it to her.

"That's a copy," he added. "The original is in the hands of the San Pedro police. They found it when they searched Mike Prescott's apartment, along with some other interesting items that should be making his life very difficult right about now."

"Mike Prescott?" Leda mumbled, accepting the paper, her eyes still on Reardon's face.

"Yeah. You remember him. He was the guy who framed me and then took off to California with my formula. He's in jail there at the moment, along with my former defense attorney and the chief engineer of the company they all worked for out there."

Leda glanced down at the note he had given her. It was a second memo in her father's handwriting, dated the same day as the first one she had seen. It countermanded the first one completely.

From: C. Bradshaw To: K. Reardon Re: Test of B-123 fuel, revised instructions. Decision on test of B-123 fuel *reversed*. Repeat, test to be conducted as per original plan. New results show compound ready for trial. Disregard earlier orders to postpone test and proceed immediately.

Her father's signature scrolled across the bottom authenticated it.

"What happened?" Leda asked, her voice barely audible.

"Prescott stole this memo to make sure that the first one, telling me not to proceed with the test, was the only one anybody saw. I received the second one and went ahead with the test, but after the accident it disappeared. Your father must have taken the first one after I was arrested, I think to try to protect me, but the other employees remembered it, and testified to its contents at the trial. That made it look like I had disobeyed orders.'' Reardon spread his hands. ''Don't you see how Prescott set me up? He made sure he had all the evidence in place to make me look guilty, and then he blew the test sky high to finish me off. And I fell right into his trap.''

''And you say my father tried to help you?''

''I think so. He knew there was a second memo, he wrote it. He kept the first one in his wallet for evidence, but he died before he could testify.''

''But why didn't Prescott destroy this?'' Leda asked, gesturing with the note in her hand.

Reardon shrugged. ''I don't know, overconfidence maybe. I had an idea he wouldn't, he had just the sort of fanatic ego that would keep the goodies around to gloat over in private. He had a whole file on me in his place, you should have seen it: correspondence from your father's company, all the plans and experiments dealing with my formula, the works.''

''He must be some kind of psychopath.''

''He's nuts, all right,'' Reardon said mildly, as if he had long accepted the mental condition of his former colleague as a fact of life.

''And you've been out in California all this time, working on this?'' Leda asked.

''That's right. I went out there and hired a private detective, and together we found out that Prescott was using my old formula, exactly as I designed it for your father's company. And guess what—no explosions. I instituted a suit for patent infringement, and then reopened the case back in Pennsylvania, charging Prescott and my old lawyer with the deaths of the people at the testing site."

"You've been busy," Leda murmured, hardly aware of what she was saying.

"Not so busy that I forgot you."

Leda sat down carefully, her mind racing. "Kyle, how could you afford to quit your job and go out to the coast, hire a detective, all of that?"

"Jim Kendall cosigned a bank loan for me," Reardon answered simply.

"He's been a good friend to you," Leda said. She hesitated before adding, in a low tone, "A far better one than I have been."

Reardon didn't answer, studying her expression.

"Why didn't you tell me any of this before now?" Leda asked, shrugging helplessly.

Reardon shook his head. "Come on, Leda, give me a break. I heard you had read the trial transcript, I could imagine what you thought. My story was incredible enough without going into missing memos and vanishing evidence. I knew how it would sound."

"You mean you knew I wouldn't believe you," Leda murmured, covering her mouth with her hand. "And so you left me alone for six months."

"No, Leda," he answered softly. "You left me."

"Because I thought you had lied to me!" Leda broke down, sobbing for the lost trust, the lost time. "Do you know how I missed you, longed for you?"

"Yes," he replied tightly. "I think I do."

"Oh, Kyle, I'm so sorry," Leda whispered, and he rushed to her side, pulling her into his arms.

"So am I, darling, so am I," he said soothingly, holding her as she released the torrent of tears she had kept inside for so long. Overcome by the mixed emotions of relief and happiness, she couldn't do anything more than cling to him and cry. He's here, she thought, he's really here, and everything is going to be all right.

Anna chose that opportune moment to enter the dressing room, humming and carrying a sandwich. She stopped in her tracks when she saw Reardon with Leda, and spun around on her heel, heading back out to the hall.

"Anna," Leda called in a strong voice, sitting up and accepting Reardon's handkerchief. "Get back in here."

Anna returned meekly, swallowing a bite of the sandwich she held. "Yes?" she said, dramatically innocent.

"Kyle here has been telling me a very interesting story," Leda said, and Anna looked at Reardon, wondering how much he had revealed.

"It seems you two have become pen pals," Leda added dryly.

Anna surrendered. "Phone pals too," she said. She grinned at Reardon. "Hi, Kyle,"

"Hi, yourself," he said, laughing.

"I should be mad at you," Leda said archly, eyeing her friend.

"Are you?" Anna asked, her ham-and-cheese poised in mid-air.

"No."

Anna winked. "I did it all in the cause of true love. It was obvious you two were crazy about each other, you just needed a little help, that's all."

"Which you provided."

"Free of charge," Anna pointed out, taking another bite.

"So what have you been telling this guy for the past six months?" Leda asked, adjusting her position within the circle of Reardon's arms.

"The details of your social life," Anna replied.

Leda stared at Reardon. "You know about all those awful dates I had?" she asked, horrified.

He nodded, smiling. "I must say I enjoyed hearing the stories."

"I'll bet," Leda said huffily, throwing Anna a black look.

"Well, I guess I'd better be going," Anna observed, edging toward the door. "I think you can carry on without me."

"Lock the door on your way out," Reardon said huskily, turning Leda to face him.

"I'll miss you too," Anna muttered, snatching up her purse as she passed. She exited quickly, fixing the lock as requested.

"Alone at last," Reardon whispered, seeking Leda's mouth with his. Silence reigned for long minutes, and then he said, "Where are you staying?"

"At a hotel a few blocks from here," Leda answered, rubbing her face against his shoulder.

"Too long to wait," Reardon pronounced. "This couch will have to do." He pulled her down with him, shifting his weight.

Leda curled luxuriously into his body, closing her eyes. "Kyle, why did you come for me, after the way I left?"

"You know the answer to that," he said, smoothing her hair with his old, familiar gesture. "I love you."

"But I lost faith in you, I really did," she murmured, unable to forgive herself for what he was able to dismiss.

"You had faith in me when no one else did," he reminded her.

"But I gave up. I gave up on you too soon."

"You found what you thought was proof that I had deceived you. I can understand your confusion. People aren't perfect, Leda, and I don't expect them to be." He kissed the side of her neck, trailing his lips along her soft skin. "Do you think you can go back to Yardley with a man who faces the task of clearing his name?"

"Of course. We'll tackle that together. With what you've accomplished already, you'll get your license back."

"Jim Kendall said I could have my old job, until I'm able to fly again." He hugged her close. "Leda, what about your aunt?"

"Don't worry about her. She's stubborn, Kyle, but she isn't stupid. When she sees the new evidence, she'll admit that she was wrong."

"I hope so," he said doubtfully.

"I love you," Leda said fiercely. "That's all that matters."

"Do you, saddle shoes?" he asked. "Do you still?"

"Oh, yes," she said softly, alarmed that he could even wonder about it. "Oh, yes." She burrowed into him, seeking the warmth and comfort that only he could give.

"Then the past is forgiven, for both of us. We start over today, okay?" he said, sliding his hands under her sweater.

Leda arched toward him, melting under his much-missed, longed-for touch.

"Okay," she whispered, surrendering to her winter lover—soon to be her husband throughout the year.

READERS' COMMENTS ON SILHOUETTE DESIRES

"Thank you for Silhouette Desires. They are the best thing that has happened to the bookshelves in a long time."

—V.W.*, Knoxville, TN

"Silhouette Desires—wonderful, fantastic—the best romance around."

—H.T.*, Margate, N.J.

"As a writer as well as a reader of romantic fiction, I found DESIREs most refreshingly realistic—and definitely as magical as the love captured on their pages."

—C.M.*, Silver Lake, N.Y.

"I just wanted to let you know how very much I enjoy your Silhouette Desire books. I read other romances, and I must say your books rate up at the top of the list."

—C.N.*, Anaheim, CA

"Desires are number one. I especially enjoy the endings because they just don't leave you with a kiss or embrace; they finish the story. Thank you for giving me such reading pleasure."

—M.S.*, Sandford, FL

*names available on request

You won't want to miss a single one of the heart-felt stories presented by Silhouette Special Edition; and when you take advantage of this special offer, you won't have to.

You'll also receive a FREE subscription to the Silhouette Books Newsletter as long as you remain a member. Each lively issue is filled with news on upcoming titles, interviews with your favorite authors, even their favorite recipes.

To become a home subscriber and receive your first 4 books FREE, fill out and mail the coupon today!

Silhouette Special Edition®

Silhouette Books, 120 Brighton Rd., P.O. Box 5084, Clifton, NJ 07015-5084

If that's the kind of romance reading you're looking for, Silhouette Intimate Moments novels were created for you.

The first 4 Silhouette Intimate Moments selections are absolutely FREE and without obligation, yours to keep! You can cancel at any time.

You'll also receive a FREE subscription to the Silhouette Books Newsletter as long as you remain a member. Its filled with news on upcoming books, interviews with your favorite authors, even their favorite recipes.

To get your first 4 Silhouette Intimate Moments novels FREE, fill out and mail the coupon today!

Silhouette Intimate Moments®

Silhouette Books, 120 Brighton Rd., P.O. Box 5084, Clifton, NJ 07015-5084

Silhouette Desire

COMING NEXT MONTH

TANGLED WEB—Lass Small
The object of an outrageous matchmaking scheme, Peggy Dillon
found herself at the mercy of a fat old dog, invisible alligators and a
man determined to win her heart.

HAWK'S FLIGHT—Annette Broadrick
Dr. Paige Winston wasn't used to the rugged life, but when she found
herself stranded in the Arizona mountains with handsome
adventurer Hawk Cameron, she had to learn fast.

TAKEN BY STORM—Laurien Blair
Teenage-advice columnist Randy Wade thought she had all the
answers, but when single parent Nick Jarros stormed into her office,
she found herself at a loss for words.

BEWITCHED—Sara Chance
Isis O'Shea possessed an unusual talent, a talent that James Leland
needed. Was his courtship of the beautiful psychic the beginning of
love or just the means to an end?

A COLDHEARTED MAN—Lucy Gordon
Accused of a crime that she had no memory of committing, Helena
knew her only defense rested in the hands of the man she loved…the
man she'd jilted ten years before.

NAUGHTY, BUT NICE—Jo Ann Algermissen
Damon Foxx was one of the socially elite, and Tamara Smith was a
"bad girl" from the wrong side of the tracks. Falling in love was
definitely against the rules!

AVAILABLE NOW:

GOLDEN GODDESS
Stephanie James

RIVER OF DREAMS
Naomi Horton

TO HAVE IT ALL
Robin Elliott

LEADER OF THE PACK
Diana Stuart

FALSE IMPRESSIONS
Ariel Berk

WINTER MEETING
Doreen Owens Malek